HILLS OF BLOOD

To the Confederate prisoners of the Civil War the offer seemed almost too good to be true: volunteer to fight the Indians and receive freedom in return. Captain Terrance saw the chance to escape the living hell of the prison and ordered his men to enlist in the special corps. Now he has the opportunity to look for the fabulous gold of the Red Hills — and to strike a blow for the South in the war which, to him, is all-important . . .

FRANK WEIGHT

HILLS OF BLOOD

Complete and Unabridged

LINFORD
Leicester

First published in Great Britain in 2000

First Linford Edition
published 2008

Originally published in paperback as
Men of the West by Chet Lawson

The moral right of the author has been asserted

British Library CIP Data

Weight, Frank, *1919* –
   Hills of blood.—Large print ed.—
   Linford western library
   1. Western stories
   2. Large type books
   I. Title II. Lawson, Chet, *1919* –. Men of
   the west
   823.9'14 [F]

   ISBN 978–1–84782–055–6

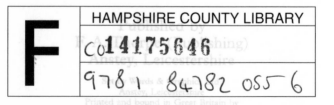

Published by
F. A. Thorpe (Publishing)
Anstey, Leicestershire

Set by Words & Graphics Ltd.
Anstey, Leicestershire
Printed and bound in Great Britain by
T. J. International Ltd., Padstow, Cornwall

This book is printed on acid-free paper

1

The place stank. It reeked with the mingled odours of rotting leather, burning clothing, burning animal fat and suppurating wounds. The air, thick and heavy, held a miasma of human suffering, an almost tangible thing which streamed from the moisture-dripping walls or rose sickly from the foul, mud-trodden straw underfoot. Air, what there was of it, came through a tiny, barred window high on one wall and a thin, guttering light came from a tin bowl which held scraps of fat and a crude wick. Once the place had held stores, sacks of grain and unfeeling tools. Now it held men.

Too many men. The broken men of the Confederacy, the men in grey who had been captured, often wounded, by the Union Forces. For this was the year 1864 and the fortunes of war were swinging from the South to the North as the men in blue pressed harder and harder against the Confederate States. It was a bitter struggle with no time for tender emotions such as pity or sympathy. Cruelty was not deliberate but was forced on the victors through necessity. Prisoners had to be held and held in a convenient place and so more and more men were thrust into the warehouse, a bale of straw thrown after them and, aside from regular supplies of food and water, were left to live or die.

It was, Captain Terrance thought, the nearest approach to hell that he had ever seen.

He sat on a heap of straw, his back against the wall, his eyes fastened on the tiny square of fading daylight beyond the barred window. Around him the bodies of men who had been flung, still covered with blood and dirt, into the warehouse, shifted and muttered in restless sleep, or sat and stared, dull-eyed, into a future which held no promise. From one corner a youth, scarcely more than a boy, wiped his harmonica and struck up *Dixie*. In this place and at this time the lilting tune seemed a mockery. It woke memories best left forgotten, the memories of graceful houses and the warm, mimosa scented night, the pale white faces of magnolias, the soft singing of the slaves after their work was done, the whole, easy, cultured life of a system which was even now being torn to pieces in the fury of war.

And yet it stirred, too, did that tune. It made the blood tingle and the feet twitch to the remembered cadences of marches when the men in grey had swung towards the north intent on teaching those damn Yankees a needed lesson. The tune had been played and sung, whistled and hummed as the cannon roared and the yelling troops had hurled themselves at barely seen men in blue and the air became full of the reek of powder and the whine of bullets.

Terrance sighed and eased his wounded arm. He had bandaged it with his shirt and, despite the dirt, it was healing well. He rubbed his hand across his lips and chin, thick with beard and crusted with dirt, ran his tongue over his teeth and tried to forget the miasma, the suffering, the over-crowded warehouse and the blank future in the oblivion of sleep. He woke at a touch on the shoulder.

'Captain.'

'What is it?' He blinked as he stared at shadows. The daylight had gone and only the guttering flame of the improvised lamp threw a dim light over the huddled bodies around him. 'Who is it?'

'Sweeny, sir.' The sergeant made a tentative salute. 'It's old Zebe, Captain. I think he's dying.'

'We're all dying,' said Terrance bitterly, but he rose to his feet. 'Is he in pain?'

'Two men are holding him down.' Sweeny stepped over prostrate figures to one corner of the warehouse. A man stared up at them, an old man, his seamed and wrinkled face making him look like a bald-headed monkey. Sweat oozed from his forehead and left little white trails over the dirt around his eyes. Two men sat beside him, their hands firm and gentle on his writhing body. Around his naked torso a crude bandage showed the old and new stains of blood.

'Zebe.' Terrance dropped on his knees beside the old man. 'Zebe, can you hear me?'

'I can hear you, Captain.' Pain distorted the seamed features. 'Water!'

'Find some water.' Terrance gave the order without looking at the sergeant. He nodded to the men holding Zebe's arms. 'Hold tight, we'll take a look at his wound.'

A Spencer ball had blasted its way into the old man's body, tearing through into the spleen and lodging against the backbone. With proper equipment and instruments Terrance thought that the old man might have stood a chance; as things were he stood no chance at all. Now that the wound had broken open again, Terrance felt a sense of terrible helplessness as he examined the thin, tough body of the old man.

'How is it?' Zebe had quietened a little during the examination.

'Rest quietly.' Terrance looked up as the sergeant came towards him, a tin cup in one hand. The light from the crude lamp cast dancing shadows against the walls and, for a moment, Terrance imagined that Sweeny was some giant ogre lurching towards them. He shook his head to rid it of the fantasy, took the water, held it to the old man's lips.

'Thanks.' Zebe rolled his head after he had gulped the stale water. 'Sure tasted good. Better than that time when I was up in the Dead Valley when I drank the water I found in the stomach of a dead mule.' He tried to chuckle, the laugh turning into a wracking cough.

'Relax,' soothed Terrance. 'Try and get some sleep.'

'I'll get some sleep,' promised the old man. 'Too much of it.' He ran his tongue over his lips. 'Water.' Terrance looked at Sweeny who shook his head.

'There ain't no more,' he said. 'Not until morning when the blue bellies bring up our ration.'

'Damn Yankees,' said the old man. He rolled his head, his eyes, fever bright, staring at Terrance. 'You're a queer one, a right man. You could have claimed officers' privileges instead of coming in here with the rest of us. Soft beds, good food, water . . . ' He licked his lips. 'Water.'

'Relax,' said Terrance.

'Sure.' Zebe stared at the dancing flame of the lamp. 'Funny, reminds me of the fires in the Lodges of the Sweet Water tribe. Stayed there when young, a long time ago now. Beaver was thick and buffalo for the asking. There was a girl, a right squaw, as pretty as paint and clever with her hands.' He sighed.

7

'What was her name now?' He shook his head. 'Slips the mind but I'll be seeing her soon now. Wonder if she'll recognize me now? Was a straight youngster when I met her, straight and with a good eye and could shoot the head off a quail at two hundred paces.' He chuckled. 'Remember the rendezvous of '27, right time then.' His head rolled and lips parted to reveal a questing tongue. 'God. I'm thirsty! Water! Water, damn you! Give me a drink!'

'Steady!' Terrance nodded to the sergeant and rose to his feet. 'Stay by him.'

'Where you going?' Sweeny stared at the captain. 'Them blue bellies won't give you nothing but a rifle butt in the face for calling them. Don't do it.'

Terrance grunted and stepped carefully towards the door. It was of solid oak, rusty with great straps of iron, pierced by a judas window and chained on the outside. He kicked at it, beat on it with his hands, the noise echoing and rolling throughout the warehouse. Men awoke, stared towards him, then sank back on the foul straw, their heavy eyes closing in apathetic sleep.

Again Terrance pounded on the door, his temper rising as he thought of the dying man and the cold indifference of their captors. After what seemed an eternity the judas window opened and a face, hard and cold, shaved and clean, stared at him.

'What you want?'

'Water.'

'Drink your own sweat,' the guard laughed. 'You damn Johnny Rebs can rot for all I care.'

'There's a dying man in here,' said Terrance tightly. 'A bucket of water won't hurt you.' His anger rose. 'Hell, man, you'd give a dog a drink. Water don't cost anything, does it?'

'Shut your mouth.'

'I want water.'

'You'll get it,' said the guard suddenly. 'I reckon I can spare some water.' He chuckled and moved away. Instinct warned Terrance and he stepped aside as a gush of foul liquid shot through the opening towards him. It was more filth than water, redolent of latrines and garbage.

'You swine!' Anger fumed within him. 'You dirty, stinking apology of a soldier!' He glared through the opening and vented his anger in a stream of abuse. The guard snarled, lifted his bayoneted rifle, and thrust the wicked point directly at the captain's face.

Reflex action saved his eyes. Pain burned in his cheek as he twisted sideways, the bayonet slashing the skin. Then his hands were moving, whipping up to clamp on the barrel of the rifle, his feet lifting to thrust against the door and, with all his strength, he tugged at the weapon. It came free, jerked out of the guard's hands, the long barrel sliding between the bars of the judas window then stuck as the bolt caught on the bars. Immediately Terrance thrust it back, driving the brass-shod butt with the full strength of his arms and body into the startled face of the guard. The soldier screamed as his nose pulped beneath the blow and went down, thrashing on the ground outside the door, the rifle clattering as it slipped through the opening.

Dabbing at his cheek Terrance returned to the dying man.

Zebe was still raving, talking of scenes of his youth when he had hunted the wide plains and mountains of the great continent. He spoke of Indian tribes now only memories, wiped out by smallpox and other diseases brought by the white man. He spoke of the great rendezvous when all the trappers had congregated to sell their furs and drink raw whiskey. He rambled about the wagon trains and the settlers, the vast herds of buffalo and the wide open places to the west and north. Then he became calm, his eyes, still fever-bright but sane, and Terrance knew that he stared at a man soon to die.

'Zebe.' He sat beside the wrinkled old man, his hands gentle as they wiped the sweat from around the creased eyes. 'Try and rest now.'

'I'm dying,' said Zebe suddenly. 'That's so, ain't it. Captain?'

Terrance nodded. He didn't believe in lying to a man about to die. Zebe was an old soldier, a man who had seen death in many forms, he didn't need the sop of lying comfort.

'I knew it.' The old man stretched, frowning against the hands which held him. 'No call to hold me down,' he wheezed. 'I don't reckon to go anywhere.'

'Pain gone?' Terrance nodded to the men and they released their grip on the old man. Sweeny, his face bitter, squatted down beside the captain.

'I've been all over,' he said. 'There ain't a drop of water in the place, not unless you want to lick the walls.' He squinted towards the old man. 'How is he?'

'Comfortable now,' said Terrance softly. 'The pain's mostly gone and his mind's clear.'

'Will he die?'

'Yes.' Terrance stooped over the lamp and adjusted the wick. It was made from a few strands of cotton twisted together and set in a reeking lump of fat. It smelt and the light was bad, but it was light and all they had. As he trimmed the wick the tiny glow brightened throwing the watching faces of the men around Zebe into sharp relief. Bearded, dirty, their eyes glistening in their gaunt features, they looked more like animals than the soldiers they were.

'There'll be trouble over what you did to that guard,' whispered Sweeny. 'I was watching and what you did was neat, but there'll be trouble.'

'He tried to jab out my eye,' said Terrance. 'He asked for what he got.'

'Sure, but they don't love us, those Yankees.' Sweeny spat. 'That guard'll get even, you'll see.' He fumbled among his rags. 'I've got me a knife hidden away. It's a small one I kept in my boot and they didn't find it when they searched me.' He produced it, a tiny sliver of steel, sharp and pointed, more a woman's weapon than a real knife but capable of killing a man if stabbed in the right place. He held it to the captain. 'You take it.'

'No.'

'Take it, Captain. You might need it.'

'Keep it.' Terrance leaned towards the lamp again. 'Killing won't do any good.'

'No?' Sweeny stared around the warehouse. 'Seems to me that if we're going to die we might as well do it like men. I'd go if I could take one of the blue bellies with me.' He spat against a wall. 'I used to keep my hogs in a better place than this. It ain't right to treat white men so.'

Terrance grunted, not agreeing, not disagreeing. He leaned forward as Zebe opened his eyes and stared around him.

'Zebe.'

'That you, Captain?'

'I'm here.' Terrance could do nothing but offer the dying man the comfort of knowing that he wasn't dying alone. He closed his big, strong hand over the thin, wasted claw. 'We're all here, Zebe.'

'That's right.' Zebe licked his lips. 'Sure wish that I had a drink.'

'You'll have a drink soon.'

'Won't need it then.' The old man hunched himself higher on the slimy straw of his bed. He stared around with feverish eyes, looked at the two men, Sweeny, finally the captain. 'Captain.'

'Yes?'

'There's something I've got to tell you before I go.'

'I'm listening.'

'It's a mine,' whispered Zebe. 'A real bonanza. I found it in the Blanca Hills not too far from Denver. You know Denver?'

'In Colorado?'

'That's the place.' Zebe coughed and a rill of blood seeped from between his lips. He wiped his mouth, stared at his hand, let it fall to his side. 'Found it years ago when I took a prospect through that part. Always kept it secret, was going back there one day and make my pile.' The wrinkled head rolled and the wasted chest heaved. 'Never did.'

'Whereabouts in the Blanca Hills?' Sweeny hunched forward, his eyes eager.

'Head south from Denver and cross the Pueblo,' whispered Zebe. 'Strike west when you hit a range of three hills looking like a triangle. Take the trail to Herman's Gorge but leave it about two miles before you hit the canyon. Turn south again and you'll find the gold about four miles on.'

'That's a hell of a direction!' Sweeny stared at Terrance then back at Zebe. 'Can't you do better than that?'

'What for? You can find it.'

'Like hell! Colorado's a big place, we could be looking from now on and never find it.'

'That's right.' Incredibly the old man grinned. 'You think I carried that secret with me so anyone could find it?' He gestured to Terrance. 'I'll tell the captain. Bend closer, Cap, my voice isn't as strong as I'd like.'

Terrance put his ear close to the old man's lips.

'Listen,' whispered Zebe. 'The gold is there right enough. I found nuggets in the Blanca Hills as big as my thumb. The directions are right but no one could find the place just from what I said. The gold is in a small gully between twin hills. You'll know them by the fact that, at sunset, the sun colours them all red. The Indians call them the Red Hills and they stand out a mile.'

'Finished?' Sweeny was impatient. 'Did he tell you, Captain?'

'He told me.' Terrance leaned back on his heels.

'Good.' The sergeant licked his lips. 'How much gold do you reckon, old timer?'

'Gold to eat,' whispered Zebe. 'Gold to burn. Gold to throw away.' His breath rasped in his throat in the parody of a chuckle. 'And Indians.'

'Indians!'

'Comanches and Apaches,' whispered the thin voice. The wasted claw lifted, fell on Terrance's hand, 'Good luck, Captain. Remember what I told you.'

'I'll remember.' Terrance leaned across the old man. 'I'll remember, and thanks.'

Zebe smiled then, abruptly, relaxed, every muscle seeming to become flaccid at the same time. Terrance rested his hand on the naked torso, felt the pulse and the great vein of the throat, then, slowly, closed the staring eyes.

Zebe was dead.

2

Major John Laurance, commander of the garrison attached to the prisoner of war camp, read the dispatch on his desk for the fourth time and then scowled at the visitor sitting opposite his desk.

'Are you serious, Colonel,' he rapped. 'Or is this someone's idea of a joke?'

'It's no joke, Major, I assure you.' Colonel Sam Austin was a tall, rangy, sun-burned man with the expression of someone who has spent most of his life in the open. He eased himself on the narrow chair and produced a cigar case. Politely he offered one to the major, lit them, blew smoke towards the maps hanging on the wall. 'You have read my orders and the orders from HQ. They are clear, I think?'

'Yes.' Laurance was grudging in his admission. 'But do you really think your plan will work?'

'I think it will.' Austin suddenly grew more serious. 'In fact it must work, the alternative is too unpleasant to dwell upon.' He leaned across the desk 'You see, Major, we aren't just fighting one war, we are fighting two. Here in the east you forget that we've another enemy beside the Confederacy. That enemy is strong, ruthless and cunning.'

'Indians.' Laurance dismissed them with a shrug. 'Savages.'

'Savages?' Austin shrugged. 'I could argue the point but it would be a waste of time. The point is that, while our forces are engaged in civil strife, the Indians are having a field day with the settlers and prospectors in the West. With our garrisons depleted by the demands of war, our forts undermanned and our patrols cut to a minimum we are at the mercy of warring tribes such as the Apache and the Comanche.' He stared at the tip of his cigar. 'We are fighting two wars, Major, one here, the other in the West.

We are losing the one in the West.'

'Ridiculous!' The major was a man trained in rigorous tradition. To him, as to most men who had never experienced the conditions on the frontier, the Indians were little more than a nuisance. He said so.

'You have peculiar ideas as to the Indian menace,' said Austin, coldly. 'If I were to tell you that for many months now all communications have ceased between east and west on all routes through New Mexico, would you still regard that as a mere nuisance? Or that forts have been attacked and destroyed, settlers killed and their farms burned and unknown numbers of prospectors scalped or tortured?' He shook his head. 'Take my word for it, Major, Indians aren't the savages you seem to think. They are smarting under various grievances and they have skilled leaders. True, they do not realize the full picture but they do know that we are withdrawing our forces from the frontier. To them that is clear indication that they are beating us in war. They are getting bolder and more dangerous each day. The solution, to me, is obvious.'

'To you,' pointed out the major. 'To others?'

'That is what I intend to find out.' Colonel Austin rose to his feet. 'Is everything in readiness?'

'Perhaps.'

'Perhaps?' The colonel looked surprised. 'I don't understand you, Major.'

'Conditions here are not as they should be,' explained the major. 'The pressure of war . . . I needn't go into details. We have few men and the few we have are not the best soldier material. For reasons of security we have had to confine the prisoners.'

'What are you trying to say, Major?'

'You will have to address them in their quarters.'

'That is to be expected.'

'Yes.' The major hesitated. 'Of course.' He led the way outside.

Few looked up at the rattling from

the door. Once a day it opened to permit the passage of food and water and, at such times, bayonetted rifles warned the prisoners to keep their distance. Today was different only in that the door was opening later than usual. Terrance, his cheek smarting from his wound, stared towards the panel as it swung open.

'Take this,' whispered Sweeny. He held out the knife. 'You may need it.'

'No.' The captain stared at the men revealed by the opening of the door. 'I don't think so.'

Sweeny grunted, they swore with surprise as the usual routine was broken. Instead of the buckets of water and sour food which was the usual ration, armed guards drove back the prisoners and two men, one of them the camp major, entered the building. The other man, wearing the uniform, and insignia of a colonel in the Union Forces, halted, his nose wrinkling as he smelt the interior of the building.

'I warned you,' said Laurance hastily.

'The conditions here aren't all to be hoped for.'

'How long have these men been here?'

'Varying times, some only a few weeks, others a few months.'

'I see.' Austin knew better than to press the question before the guards and witnesses. He stared at the ravaged faces, the near-naked bodies and the glittering eyes facing him and took a deep breath. His plan was perhaps a wild one but he felt certain that it was the answer to his problem. But others did not think the same and reluctant permission had been granted only after much wire-pulling and friendly influence. And there was a catch, either he succeeded here or not at all.

'Men of the Confederate Army,' he began. 'You are prisoners of war taken in accordance with the laws of war and as such are entitled to certain rights, among them being the fact that you cannot be requested to do anything harmful against your cause.' He paused, wishing he dared light a cigar and knowing that to do so would be a fast way to lose the sympathy of the prisoners.

'I am not here to ask you to harm your own. I am here to offer you a chance to serve this country of ours in a dignified and lawful manner. I speak of the West, the great lands beyond the Mississippi, the lands we are trying to settle and the Indians who are waging war on us. The North has had to withdraw troops from the frontier and thus left those we must protect open to massacre by Indians. We, at this time, cannot spare troops to garrison the forts or engage on patrols against the Indians.'

He paused, letting his eyes drift over the watching men, seeing the masked hate and anger against the uniform he was wearing plain in their expressions.

'My proposal is simply this. That you agree to wear Union Blue, enlist in a special corps of the Union Army, a corps which will be solely engaged in

protecting the frontier from the depredations of the Indians, and serve as
men and soldiers in the defence of your
country, both North and South.'

'Wear blue belly uniform!' Sweeny
spat on the foul straw. 'Like hell!'

'Join the Union Army!' Another man
threw back his head and laughed. 'Man,
within three months there ain't going to
be a Union Army, not when General
Lee gets to work on it.'

Other men added their comments
and their reactions to the proposal.
Austin heard them out in silence.

'Listen,' he said. 'I am not asking you
to fight against the South, to become
renegades. I am asking you to fight our
common enemy, the Indians. The West
is starved for men and, no matter what
happens in the East, once the Indians
clear away the settlers we both suffer.
Texas is a Confederate State and Texas
is threatened by the Apache. Some of
you may have wives and children in
Texas or some other western state.
Think of them if not of yourselves.'

Listening to him Terrance had to admit Austin spoke well. He had a sincerity about him not to be found in most men. He spoke from his heart, saying what he felt to be really important and wasted no time on words or flag-waving or on false sentiment.

'Your lives, as prisoners of war, are hard,' he continued. 'I offer you freedom from these walls and conditions and, in return, I ask your oath that you will obey your officers and conduct yourselves as soldiers. The term of your enlistment will expire three months after the cessation of hostilities. You will be paid regular wages and wear regular uniform. You will eat and live like men instead of caged animals.'

'Go to hell,' yelled Sweeny. 'We ain't no renegades!' He turned to the other prisoners. 'Let's show him, shall we boys? Lemmy, where's that mouth box of yours? Ready! Go!' His arm swept down and, together to the tune from the harmonica, the roaring words of the Southern battle song echoed through

27

the warehouse. The song to which the men in grey marched and died, killed and were killed, the Southern answer to the popular *Yankee Doodle* of the North.

Terrance waited until they were in the final chorus, waited until they had ended the song and were about to repeat it. He lifted his hand.

'Silence!'

A few men ignored him and Lemmy, with his harmonica, defied the captain.

'Silence!' The iron voice of command rang throughout the building. Terrance turned and stared at the Union colonel.

'May I speak?'

Austin nodded.

'We have a man in here who has been dead for two days. During that time we have had no food, no water. Our conditions are as you see, little better for pigs than men. This is the treatment we have received at your hands. Can we expect anything better?'

'If you volunteer . . .'

'Forget that. I am talking about here

and now.' Terrance stepped forward. 'Well?'

Austin glanced at the major, waiting for him to speak. Laurance fingered his throat, coughed, then shrugged his shoulders.

'I asked a question,' said Terrance, tightly. 'I am waiting for an answer.'

'You may remove your dead,' said the major. 'Water and food will be given you.'

'And clothes, medicines, bandages?'

'Water and food will be given you.' Laurance stepped towards the door. 'Colonel?'

'A moment.' Austin stared hard at Terrance. 'Are you an officer?'

'I am, yes.'

'Then why are you here? Officers have different quarters and are entitled to better conditions.'

'If my men are good enough to fight and die with, then they are good enough to suffer with.' Terrance stared at the tall colonel. 'I remain with my men.'

'I see.' Austin bit his lips. 'Could I have a word with you in private?'

'Anything you wish to say may be said now.'

'I was going to suggest that you examine my proposition,' said Austin. 'As an officer and a gentleman I expect you to take the word of a fellow officer. I do not like to see good men waste their lives behind prison walls when they could be using them for the greater good.' He stepped forward. 'Please, a word in your ear.'

Terrance hesitated, then shook his head.

'Very well.' Austin drew himself to his full height. 'I say only this. Out West there is a new land, a big, clean, free land. That land is ours and we want to keep it ours. It is yours and mine, it belongs to the South and the North, it will be the place to which men will turn when the war is over. I ask you to think of that, I ask you to remember that we are fighting for something bigger than the right to keep slaves. We are both of us, in our own way, fighting for the right to be free. But also we have a common enemy, the Indian. I ask you to make the Indian your enemy and help to protect the innocent from the scalping knife and tomahawk.' He hesitated, looking at them.

'The concept is new and may take a while to grasp,' he said. 'I will give you time to consider. Tomorrow I shall be ready to swear in any volunteers.' He turned towards the door, hesitated just outside. 'Forget your hate of the Union,' he said seriously. 'You will not be helping the Union, you will be helping all of us, your own people and your own cause.' He turned on his heel, the major followed him, the guards stepped back and the thick, heavy door slammed back into place.

'Blue belly!' Sweeny shook his fist at the panel. 'Go to hell!' He turned to Lemmy. 'Let's give it to them. Lemmy, get out that harmonica of yours.'

'Sure, sergeant.' Lemmy grinned, wiped his battered mouth organ and began to play. The men joined in, almost a hundred voices yelling their defiance and, for a time, hunger, thirst, wounds and hardship were forgotten as they lost themselves in song.

Terrance didn't sing. He sat, face thoughtful, staring up at the tiny square of daylight high against the wall. From time to time he glanced towards the still, barely wrapped body of old Zebe, still waiting to be carried outside. He waited until the singing had died, the men collapsing wearily on the foul straw, sinking again into the apathy from which they had been aroused.

'Sergeant!'

'Yes, sir.' Sweeny saluted and came to his side. 'You want me, sir?'

'Sit down.' Terrance waited until the sergeant had settled himself. 'How long to winter, Sweeny?'

'I'm not sure.' The sergeant frowned. 'Maybe four, five months.'

'It was late spring when I was taken,' said Terrance. 'That was two months ago. The cold weather should start in about three months' time.' He glanced around the damp warehouse. 'It gets cold in these parts, in five months we'll be snow- and ice-bound.'

'Will we?' Sweeny shrugged, then nodded. 'Guess you're right.'

'You haven't a very good imagination, have you, sergeant?' Terrance drew one finger down the wall and stared at the moisture he had collected. 'We haven't got any stoves in here and no way to set them up if we had. The guards won't give us water or clothing, will they give us fuel? Winter, sergeant, ice inside and out, and us with rags instead of uniforms, wet straw to sleep on, no heat, little light.' He looked at Sweeny. 'Do I have to go on?'

'They wouldn't do it,' said the sergeant. He had grown pale. 'They wouldn't treat a slave that way.'

'Maybe not, but we aren't slaves. We're slave owners, Johnny Rebs, Southern Scum. They don't care what happens to us. And there's another thing.' He paused, letting his words gain emphasis through the silence. 'We're losing the war.'

'Like hell we are!'

'Relax, sergeant,' said Terrance quietly. 'I'm no renegade so don't talk to me as if I were. I'm an officer and I've eyes and a brain. You know as well as I do how hard things have been getting lately. Little ammunition, poor clothing, scant food, irregular payments, things like that. You've been home on a short leave and seen how tight things were getting. The South is fighting a lost cause, sergeant, and we all know it — but daren't admit it.'

'We will win the war,' said Sweeny doggedly. 'We've got to win.'

'In any war someone has got to lose,' said Terrance, quietly. 'It may be us or it may be the North. I hope that General Lee will smash the Union forces and President Jackson kick old Lincoln into the sea. That's what I'd like to happen, want to happen, but I can't blind myself to the obvious. It may not happen. We may be beaten. From what that colonel said I think we are being beaten.'

'How?' Sweeny frowned as he thought about it. 'He appealed for us to help him. Is that the talk of a winner?'

'He said that the forts and garrisons of the frontier were being stripped of men.' Terrance stared at the high window. 'They are risking everything on a crushing attack. They are collecting all their forces for one great onslaught against the South. They wouldn't do that unless they knew that there was a good chance of the North winning the war.' He looked at the sergeant.

'The South has stretched its resources as far as they will go. Every landowner has ruined himself to pour money into the war chest to keep up the flow of guns and ammunition. We almost won in the first two years, almost. We surged out and it was luck that we were held back, never mind that. The point is this, the North, because it holds the indus-trial area, can make cannon where we have to buy them. They can make ammu-nition in quantities five times greater than we can. They have more men, more material and, more important of all, they have the gold of the West to pour into their war effort.'

'What is this,' said Sweeny. 'A lecture?'

'No, a reason.'

'A reason for what?'

'For volunteering for Austin's special corps.'

'Are you serious?' Anger darkened the sergeant's features. 'Look, captain, if this is your idea of a joke then it ain't funny. No, sir. It ain't funny at all.'

'I agree.' Terrance drew his finger down the wall again and looked at the moisture on his hand. 'Three months,' he said softly. 'Cold weather and then we'll really know what hell is like.'

'No, sir.' Sweeny shook his head. 'The blue bellies may be bad but they can't be that bad. No one could.'

'Would you bet on it?' Terrance held the sergeant's eyes with his own. 'I saw a burning once,' he said gently. 'Someone claimed that a slave had stolen something, a knife I think it was. He beat the slave with a rawhide whip and, when the darkie couldn't stand it any longer, he grabbed at the thong. He was in pain, terrified, ready for anything so he tripped up his owner and ran away. They caught him and they burned him.' Terrance stared at the tense face of the sergeant.

'They tied him up and covered him with tar and then set light to it. I was a kid at the time but I've never forgotten his screams. Men, white men, stood around and laughed and made bets as to how long he would last. White men did that, Sweeny. Would they hesitate at leaving their enemies without fuel?'

'We're prisoners of war.'

'And maybe Major Laurance lost a son or a brother in the fighting. Maybe he likes us as much as those white men liked that slave. They didn't hate him, sergeant, they just didn't care. You think that Laurance will care about us?'

'I don't know,' said Sweeny. 'I just don't know.'

'Three months,' said Terrance softly, 'and half of us will be dead. Six months and only a few will be alive. You want to gamble that you'll be one of them?'

'Stop it.' The sergeant swallowed, his face glistening with sweat. 'You trying to talk me into turning traitor?'

'No.'

'That's what we'll be if we volunteer,' protested the sergeant. 'That colonel said that we wouldn't be helping the Union but what else will we be doing? If we sign up for his special corps then that will release more men for the fighting.' He stared at the captain. 'It will, won't it?'

Terrance didn't answer.

'So it's going to be tough this winter.' Sweeny shrugged. 'Hell, we ain't children, we can take it.'

'Anyone can take it,' said Terrance quietly. 'Sometimes it takes guts to be able to give it too.'

'Guts?'

'Guts and brains.' The captain touched the wound on his cheek.

'Personally I'd rather be on the giving end of the deal. I don't favour staying here to rot when there's a chance of getting out into the sunshine again.'

'I don't get it,' said Sweeny. He was baffled. 'You're a Confederate officer and you're talking like a Yankee lover. What's got into you?'

'Maybe the stink of this place,' said Terrance calmly. 'Maybe the wanting to get astride a horse again and breathe real air instead of this filth. Maybe I want to do what I can while I can for the sake of the uniform I wear.'

'You ain't a traitor,' said the sergeant. 'Not you, not in a million years.' He scowled, his forehead creased as he thought about it. Terrance's warning as to the coming winter frightened him a little. He could guess what the prison would be like without heat or extra clothing and, despite his words, he wasn't too sure that the major would provide them. He looked at the silent bundle lying in the far corner of the long, narrow building and swore with sudden bitterness.

'Gold,' he said. 'Tons of gold. And what good is it to us?'

He stared at Terrance and, at what he saw in the captain's eyes, became thoughtful.

'You said the South was in the way of losing the war.' He spoke more to himself than to the other man. 'You said that the North had more men and guns and gold. We ain't got no gold to buy cannon, but if we had?' He looked at Zebe again. 'Gold,' he whispered. 'Tons of gold.'

'Circulate among the men,' said Terrance. 'Tell them to volunteer for this project. Tell them not to be too eager and tell them this. I'm their officer, now and for always. They fight for the South, now and for always. No matter what happens they do as I say and do it to the death. Understand?'

'Sure.' The sergeant's eyes gleamed in the thickening dusk. 'Think it will work?'

'Think what will work?'

'The plan, what you've got in mind.'

'I've got nothing in mind,' said Terrance coldly. 'You don't know what you're talking about.'

'No?' Sweeny winked. 'All right, if that's the way you want it. But you gave me reasons, captain, and I'm not so dumb as I might be.' He chuckled. 'Neat, very neat.' He moved as if to climb to his feet, his mouth opening. He closed it as the captain's hand clamped on his arm.

'Sit down.'

'What? But I thought — ?'

'Sit down.' Terrance pulled the sergeant down beside him. 'Listen, how many of these men do you trust?'

'Trust? Why, all of them. They're all Confederates ain't they?'

'Are they?' Terrance shrugged. 'I doubt it. Laurance would be a fool unless he arranged to have a spy in here with us, but never mind that. Here are your orders. Drift among the men, quietly, casually. Mention the coming winter and what we can expect. Don't order anyone to volunteer but let it be known that several others are thinking about it. Say nothing about anything else.'

'But you said — '

'I know what I said. You tell that to only a few, Lawson, Lemmy, Young, Hertzman, men we can trust. The rest will learn later. Prime a few and tell them to spread the word among the others. Say nothing other than it's going to be a bad winter. Understand?'

Sweeny nodded.

3

It was good to be in the saddle again. It was good to feel the wind and sun and the comforting touch of whole uniform. And if the uniform were blue instead of grey and carried the plainness of a trooper's dress instead of the insignia of a captain that couldn't be helped. Terrance sat his mount as to the manner born, looking ahead to where the line of soldiers wended their way over the scrub and sun-browned grass of the plains. Beside him Sweeny, no longer a sergeant but a cavalryman like the rest, muttered at the plodding discipline and the freshfaced Union troops with whom they rode.

'Schoolboys,' he snorted. 'Still wet behind the ears. And they carry the guns.'

Terrance smiled, saying nothing. Far ahead the tall figure of Colonel Austin and the shorter one of Major Perlis headed the column. The major was fresh from West Point, a young graduate who had had the bad luck to provide a target for a Confederate marksman and would limp all his life as a reminder to keep down when under fire. His wound had earned him the dubious honour of being the colonel's second in command at the isolated fort deep in Indian territory.

Sweeny twisted in his saddle, staring back at the line of mounted men, the outriders and the lumbering military wagons loaded with supplies for the fort.

'Know the name of the place we're going to, Captain?'

'Fort Ambrick, and don't call me captain.'

'I forgot.' Sweeny grinned. 'Terry seems kind of familiar if you know what I mean, sir.'

'Terry it will be while we're troopers together.' Terrance shaded his eyes, looking ahead. Before them and to either side the rolling prairie stretched beneath the burning sun. A few dots far towards the horizon showed the presence of buffalo and a thin wisp of smoke reaching like a grey finger towards the sky marred the smooth expanse of the cloudless heavens. Sweeny stared towards it then at the captain.

'Smoke signal?'

'That's right.' Terrance looked back at the column. 'A long way off, further than you'd think, but it shows that some of the red devils are watching us.'

'Will they attack?'

'I doubt it. The column is too strong and Austin seems to know what he's doing.'

'Does he?' Sweeny laughed, a short, hard sound without real mirth and Terrance guessed at what he was thinking.

The volunteering had gone without a hitch. Austin, true to his word, had given the prisoners twenty-four hours to think it over and, when he had spoken to them again, had betrayed his eagerness to enrol them in his special corps. It had been a night without water or food, the second night so spent and the men were desperate. Terrance thought that the withholding of the rations had been deliberate but it had fitted into his plan. After the tall colonel had spoken no one had moved. He had pleaded again.

'I know what you are thinking,' he had said. 'You have sworn an oath to the Confederacy and you want to keep that oath. I understand and respect you for it. But I am not asking you to break it. I am asking you to fight a common enemy.' He had said more, much more and then, when he had paused, a man had stepped forward. It was inevitable that one of the prisoners would seek to escape the living hell of the warehouse and Terrance didn't blame the man for it one bit. He wouldn't have blamed him even if he had been a true Confederate but, knowing how he himself would operate, he guessed the man to be a planted spy. He, as well as Sweeny, had been circulating among the men during the night.

But it had started a small rush to volunteer. Terrance had held his own men back, knowing that eagerness would arouse suspicion but, in the end, he had signalled to Sweeny to step forward and, after further talk from the colonel, had volunteered himself. But before he could do so he'd had to agree to the loss of his rank and to accept the pay and rations of a common soldier.

Most of the men had been rejected as physically unfit but a round thirty of them had passed, all free of any but minor wounds, and had been bathed, shaved, dressed in Union blue and sent by rail to the West. There they had been met by a column of cavalry, given mounts and supplies and had struck across the prairie towards the distant fort which they, together with twice their number of raw Union recruits, would hold against the Indians.

Terrance smiled as he rode, half his

mind on what he was doing, the other half on the future. He looked up as Major Perlis came riding down the line towards him.

'Terrance.'

'Yes, sir?'

'Colonel Austin wants a word with you.' The major rode back to the head of the line and, after a moment, the captain followed him. He found Austin staring towards the horizon where the smoke lifted like a warning finger.

'You ever fight Indians, Terrance?'

'Had a brush or two with them back before the war.'

'What do you make of that signal?'

'Hunting party sending word that we're coming,' said Terrance immediately. 'Nothing to worry about.'

'That's what I thought.' Austin stared ahead. 'Mind telling me why you think that?'

'A war party would be a lot closer and so would the signal. If they were calling up more braves for the attack the column wouldn't be unbroken, it would rise in puffs. Then there's the buffalo. The Indians are probably doing some hunting to get meat and hides for the winter.' Terrance stared around him. 'This is Comanche country, isn't it?'

'That's right.'

'I thought so. Great Bear still chief?'

'No. He died last winter. Painted Horse is the chief now.' Austin stared at the man riding at his side. 'You know him?'

'Not me.' Terrance smiled. 'Just that I once traded with Great Bear. Stayed with his people a couple of seasons and did some prospecting and trading among the tribes. That was before the treaty got broken and he began collecting scalps.' He shrugged. 'Can't say that I blame him for that, I reckon that he got a pretty raw deal.'

'You don't deal with savages,' snapped Major Perlis. 'You exterminate them.'

'Do you?' Terrance stared at the major. 'Like the Confederate States maybe?'

'Rebel scum!' The major winced as

he shifted in the saddle. 'Slavers, the lot of them.'

'That's enough of that talk!' Colonel Austin glared at his second in command. 'Remember that a third of our men are from the South.'

'They should have stayed there,' said the major bitterly. 'Six feet deep for preference or dangling on a rope.' He looked at Austin. 'All right, so I know that we've got Southerners among us. I said it was a mistake and I still say so. Once they get their hands on weapons we'll be fighting a new civil war out here in the West. You can't trust them an inch.'

'I think we can,' said the colonel. He looked at Terrance. 'Is my faith justified?'

'We swore an oath,' said the captain slowly. 'You saw fit to administer it. If you didn't think that we'd keep it then why bother?' He looked at the major. 'Seems to me,' he said quietly, 'that whoever shot you should have been hung for not doing a good job. The only way to make a rattler harmless is to kill it good, wounding it only makes it meaner than before.'

'Terrance!' Austin's voice was the crack of a whip. 'Must I remind you that you are addressing your superior officer?'

'Superior?' The look he gave the major brought the blood to Perlis's face. 'Sorry, Colonel, I guess you're right.' Terrance gave a salute. 'Your permission to leave?'

'Granted.'

Austin stared after the captain as he rode back down the line, watching the way the big, broad man held his reins and sat in his saddle. He hadn't really wanted to speak to him at all, just examine him now that he was away from the prison and had grown used to the taste of freedom. He sighed and stared before him as he guided the column over the prairie.

Terrance was going to be a problem. He was a good man, hard, a skilled soldier and would be invaluable in patrolling the country if — ? Austin knew the fanaticism of the South, the ideals of honour and duty and the cause which prompted the Confederate Army. They fought like madmen for what they considered to be their rights and the justice for which they had gone to war. But for them, now, the war was over. It had been replaced by a new war — the long, blood-stained struggle to turn a wilderness into a civilized community. It was the dream for which Austin had fought all his life, from the day he had watched his parents die in a burning cabin while the Indians had whooped and shrieked as they destroyed and scalped men, women and children.

Later he had learned that the Indians had not been wholly to blame. White traders selling poisonous whiskey had inflamed the braves to the point where they had literally gone mad with blood lust, the fumes of the vile spirits dulling their human instincts. But the traders had been white and so had to be protected. The Indians, as always, suffered in burned villages and dead warriors.

Austin started as he became aware that Perlis was speaking.

'What? What did you say?'

'How far to the fort, Colonel?'

'We'll be there before sundown.' Austin glanced up at the sun. 'About two hours.'

'Can't be too soon for me.' Perlis shifted in his saddle, the pain from his crippled leg making him irritable. 'When we get there, what happens?'

'We relieve the garrison for front-line duty.' Austin didn't want to talk about it. Perlis did.

'Lucky devils,' he said enviously. 'They'll get swift promotion in the war while we'll be forgotten stuck in this wilderness.' He touched the holstered pistol at his side. 'Makes a man wish for action so that he could clean up the Indians and get back to civilization.'

'You'll see action,' said Austin grimly. 'Too much of it if I'm not mistaken. Best to hope that you see none at all.'

Perlis grunted, obviously not agreeing with Austin's sentiments and, for the sake of something to do, rode back down the line yelling harsh orders to close up and look like soldiers instead of stuffed dummies. Austin watched him go, feeling again the anger he had felt at being given such an unsuitable officer as his second in command. And yet he'd had no choice. It had taken all his influence to retain a garrison at Fort Ambrick at all — the Indian Bureau seemed to think that the West could look after itself and that the Indians had been tamed for all time. Austin and the settlers who depended on the protection of the cavalry knew just how far the Indians had been tamed.

He stared again at the column of smoke, knowing that, somewhere towards the horizon, keen eyes were watching his every move, as Indian scouts, moving with practised ease, moved alongside the column like drifting ghosts. He shrugged off the feeling, twitched at the reins of his horse and speeded up the passage of the column a little. He knew that he wouldn't feel really comfortable until he reached the thick log stockade of the fort.

Behind him the men and wagons also speeded up, Perlis shouting harsh orders while the sergeants, attempting to whip their inexperienced men into some kind of military order, repeated the orders with colourful oaths. One of them, a squat, thick-armed man with a scarred cheek and tobacco stained moustache, reined alongside Terrance and Sweeny.

'Hi, Rebs,' he said. 'Like the trip?'

'Could be worse.' Sweeny spat in the dust. 'Nothing like a taste of gaol to make a man appreciate the sun and good company.'

Gilcross laughed. He was a man who never tormented himself with thoughts other than those needed to remain alive. Unlike the majority of the column he had no deep feeling one way or the other against his late enemies. They were soldiers, he was a soldier, and that was that. He was also a Westerner and had spent his life on the prairies. He reached for his canteen.

'Seen the smoke?'

'We saw it.'

'Guy down the line asked me what it was. I told him it was the cooking fires from the fort and he believed me.' The sergeant laughed at his own humour. 'Wait until these babies hear a war whoop or two and see a Comanche coming at them with a tomahawk. Like to bet I won't have to shoot a couple to stop the rest from running away?'

'Would you?' Terrance stared at the man and read his answer. 'You would.'

'Sure I would.' Gilcross dismissed the question with a shrug. 'Where you from?'

'Richmond,' said Terrance. 'Heard of it?'

'The Capitol of the South; sure I have.' Gilcross smiled at a pleasant memory. 'Was there once five, six years back. Went to New Orleans, too. Now there's a place for a man to have himself some fun.' He chuckled. 'Saw a duel while I was there. A couple of Creoles fell out over a dame and decided to settle things the hard way. They tied their left wrists together and took a bowie apiece in their right hand. They waited for the word and then went at each other like a couple of wildcats.' He grunted and shook his head. 'I had a bet on one of them but he let me down. Took nine inches of steel in the belly and lost his life, the fight, and my hopes of a big pot.'

'And the other?' Sweeny was interested.

'He collected it, too, right in the ticker. In fact they both cashed in their chips at the same time.' Gilcross sucked at his teeth. 'Come to think of it, I never did find out who finally won the dame.'

'What made you join the army?' Sweeny waved his hand at the prairie. 'Seems as if they'd have a hard time finding you to tell you there was a war on at all if you was to stay out here all the time.'

'I lived near the fort,' said Gilcross, apparently unaware of Sweeny's sarcasm. 'When they asked me to join I reckoned that I might as well draw free rations and ammunition as well as getting paid for what I'd have to do anyways. So I signed on with the colonel.'

'Colonel Austin?'

'That's the one.' Gilcross nodded towards the head of the column. 'I used to scout and hunt for him, kept his men supplied with meat when they was building the fort.' He sighed, wiped his mouth and took another drink from the canteen. He shook it, listened to it, sighed again and emptied it. Terrance caught the scent of whiskey and guessed that Gilcross had broken regulations and filled his canteen with alcohol instead of water.

'What do you think of the colonel?' asked Terrance. Information, any and all information was of use. The more he could learn the better and Gilcross seemed to know quite a bit about the colonel.

'He's a good man,' said the sergeant. 'A real good man.'

'We're all good men,' said Sweeny. 'All God's chillun. I've heard the darkies sing that a hundred times if I've heard them once.'

'You own slaves?' Gilcross looked at Sweeny.

'A couple. Why?'

'Did you?' The sergeant stared at Terrance.

'You can't grow cotton without using slaves to pick it,' said the captain. 'Certainly I owned slaves, still own them as far as I know.'

'You won't for long,' said the sergeant grimly. 'That's what this war's all about.'

'Is it?' Terrance shrugged. 'All I know is that the North didn't want us to live our own lives. We didn't want to obey the North. What has the owning of slaves to do with it?'

'Maybe nothing.' Gilcross frowned as he tried to think about it. 'But it seems kind of wrong for one man to own

59

another. Don't seem natural.'

'I agree.' Terrance smiled at the sergeant. 'But what could I do? The slaves came to me when my father died and I was stuck with them. To work the plantation I needed labour and the only labour I could get was slave labour. I couldn't set them free, if I had then they would have starved or been sold again into slavery. I had whole families dependent on me, old men, women, young babies as well as young and old workers. All I could do was to continue to own them, let them work for me to find the money I needed to pay for their food and cabins, and try to see some way out of the tangle.'

'Tough,' said Gilcross.

'It was a problem,' admitted Terrance.

'Then why did you fight?' Gilcross was still trying to think things out. 'If you didn't believe in slavery then why go to war about it?'

'That's different.'

'How come? You could have stayed at home.'

'So could you,' pointed out the captain. 'You didn't, why?'

'The colonel wanted me to join so I did.' To Gilcross it was simple.

'My colonel wanted me to join in the same way,' smiled Terrance. 'Shall we leave it at that?'

'Why not?' Gilcross lifted himself in his stirrups and stared back along the line. 'Look at those wagons! If they get much further behind they'll be in the next State.' He rode off, yelling curses at the wagon drivers and forcing them to whip up their mules so as to remain with the column. Sweeny stared after him, then at Terrance.

'You thinking of what I'm thinking?'

'Maybe.'

'I lay money that you are.' Sweeny grinned. 'Give me twenty of the old bunch and I'd cut this column to ribbons. Look at the way we're riding! Talk about sitting ducks!'

'They'll learn.'

'Sure they'll learn, but will they be allowed to live long enough to do it?'

Sweeny glowered towards the rising column of smoke. 'If I was an Indian sitting up there and watching us down here I'd have me a ball. Ride straight in, cut off the wagons, hit the column coming and going and it'll be all over. And us with no guns.'

'We'll get guns,' said Terrance. 'They'll arm us at the fort.'

'The fort!' Sweeny spat. 'If it's still standing.'

'It is.' Terrance pointed ahead. 'See? There it is.'

Like a trailing snake the column moved across the prairie towards the squat shape of Fort Ambrick.

4

Painted Horse, chief of the Comanche, sat on his horse and stared below. He stood on a high bluff rearing above wooded slopes which fell away to the winding ribbon of the Pueblo River, narrow here near its source and turbulent with hidden rocks. To the west the high ramparts of The Rockies reached for the sky and the jagged summits of the Blanca Hills thrust snow-capped peaks towards the blazing sun.

The chief of the Comanche was a tall, lithe warrior, his naked arms bearing the thin, white lines of old scars. He was no longer young yet still retained the grace and agility of youth. He wore a sleeveless tunic of soft deerskin ornamented with beads, trousers of the same material fringed and beaded to match the tunic. Moccasins clothed his feet and a belt around his waist supported knife and tomahawk. Even though he wore no paint and was not on the warpath, he carried, as all Indians did, his weapons of war. Apart from the knife and tomahawk he had a bow slung over his shoulders and a quiver stuffed full of arrows. The bow was of horn, the string of sinew, the arrows painted and feathered to his individual taste. They were hunting arrows, not the wickedly barbed ones used for war, for such arrows ripped and tore the flesh and spoilt the game. In his hands he held a rifle, a Spencer carbine similar to those used by the cavalry, its sleek modernness at strange variance with the small, round shield of buffalo hide which hung from the saddle. The shield was both symbolical and a sign of valour. The owner of such a shield believed it able to protect him from all harm and yet, to win the right to carry such a shield, he had first to prove his courage and skill in war. Painted Horse carried it, not because he believed the tough hide could turn a bullet which, at long range it could, but because he was a Comanche and a chief of Comanches and to carry the shield was a thing expected by his warriors.

His horse moved, stamping at the soft ground with an impatient hoof, not whinneying, for Indian ponies were trained never to whinney. Painted Horse patted the neck of his mount and stared again at what he saw below.

'Many Long Knives,' Red Dog, a scarred veteran of many battles, grunted as he stated the obvious. Behind him sat a half dozen warriors, none wearing warpaint, all members of the hunting party which had signalled the approach of the column.

'Boys,' said Painted Horse. His keen eyes had seen the fresh faces and awkward bearing of the new arrivals.

'A boy can use the weapons of the white man,' reminded Red Dog. 'It takes no courage to kill from a distance.'

The Indians grunted their agreement. They liked the rifles because it made the killing of game easy and provided much meat and hides for their wigwams, but, in war, they preferred to meet their enemies hand to hand.

'It was said,' continued Red Dog, 'that we had beaten the Long Knives and were sweeping them back into the sea. This was said by the Cheyenne and the Apache, by the Sioux and the Pawnees. Those words were true words for the Long Knives left our lands and their forts wasted in idleness. Now they return.'

'Those words were the talk of fools,' said Painted Horse evenly. 'Never do the white men yield what they have taken.'

'Yet they left and did not return.'

'They left,' agreed the chief. 'But they did not all leave. The men with hair on their faces stayed to collect the yellow stone from our hills. The men with the firewater stayed to steal our senses and take our furs. Those who dig the ground with sticks and act as squaws to cattle stayed. Only the Long Knives left, and not all. It seems that the wise men of the Nations read sign where there was no sign to read.'

'We will make them all leave,' said Red Dog. 'We will win again these lands which our fathers left us. We will fight and the white men will die.'

Grunts echoed his words as the listening Indians signalled their agreement.

'Talk kills no buffalo,' said Painted Horse dryly. 'The boasting of children collects no scalps. Squaws go hungry while men tell of the great deeds they intend to do — one day.'

'You mock?' Red Dog edged his pony closer to the chief. 'You laugh at the words of Red Dog?'

'Red Dog is a brave warrior,' said the chief calmly. 'In battle he is the first to kill and his coup are many. Can a man have such courage and the wit of Manitou at the same time?'

'You talk with the words of a snake,' said the scarred warrior admiringly. 'Your words are the words of the soft winds which cool the fever and they are as the running water which quenches the thirst. They are as the shield to turn away the arrows of anger.'

'They are words,' said Painted Horse shortly. 'The hard thrown spear is an argument no words can vanquish.' He leaned forward in his saddle. 'The Long Knives are marching again.'

'Not the same ones.' Red Dog shaded his eyes. 'Boys entered the fort but men come out.'

The Indians watched silently as the long column of relieved troops swung from the fort and headed towards the east. They rode with the skill of long practice, their polished leather boots and saddles, scabbards and belts glistening in the light of the dying sun. They rode with mechanical precision, a close-knit body of experienced fighting men armed and ready for any action.

'More come out than went in,' mused Red Dog. 'Why is that?'

'The boys are to garrison the fort,' said Painted Horse. 'The men are riding towards the rising sun away from our lands.'

'Shall we attack?'

'No. We should die beneath their guns and it would be a foolish thing to do. They are riding away and soon will be out of our lands. The boys will remain.' He swung his mount away from the fort. 'We ride.'

They rode as Indians rode, without saddles, their legs gripping the sturdy bodies of their mounts as they leaned forward. Beneath them the unshod hooves thudded on the seared grass and, aside from the soft beat of the hooves and the faint sounds of moving equipment, they rode in silence.

It began to grow dark as the sun slipped beneath the horizon and, when at last they came to the village, the sky was black and glittering with stars. Painted Horse dismounted, led his horse into the corral, called a young boy to tend it and walked to his wigwam. His squaw was waiting for him with a smoking pot of food and he ate hungrily, dipping his hands into the mess of beans and meat, lifting handfuls to his mouth and wiping the grease from his hands on to his arms. Red Dog joined him as he finished the meal.

'We have a prisoner,' he said. 'A white man.' He folded his arms and waited for Painted Horse to speak.

'Who took the white man prisoner?'

'Black Eagle.'

'I will speak with Black Eagle.'

Black Eagle was a young warrior, the son of Red Dog, though, as he was a man, each referred to the other by name. Indian children, during their early years, were given everything they wanted, never punished and showered with affection from every member of the tribe. The result was that every Indian had a tremendous sense of belonging, of being wanted, a part of the communal life. No Indian was ever troubled by a sense of insecurity. As a means of freeing an individual from fears and doubts the method of upbringing was the best ever devised but the results, aside from individual stability, led to a refusal to accept discipline in any shape or form. A father, once his son had passed his initiation and become a man entitled to ride the warpath, with the other warriors, no longer mentioned him by other than his proper name. A son, on the other hand, felt no sense of duty towards his parents, more than to anyone else. Affection, yes, but not duty.

Black Eagle nodded to his father and stared at Painted Horse.

'You took the white man prisoner?'

'Yes.'

'Why?'

'Because it was my will,' said the young warrior hotly. Painted Horse smiled.

'To ask the reason for an action is not to condemn it,' he said quietly. 'But perhaps you think that you should be chief in my place?'

Soft as the words were they constituted a challenge. Black Eagle, if he wished, could meet the challenge and appeal to the tribe. If they backed him then Painted Horse would be deposed in favour of the new chief. But for such a young, untried warrior to challenge such a great chief would be the height of madness. He would be scorned and made the butt of jeers and would either have to take his belongings and leave the tribe or meet his taunters in mortal combat. Painted Horse, well aware that the youth knew the customs of the tribe as well as he did, had mentioned the challenge only to remind the young warrior that he was chief and that, while his word was far from law, his position and the many coup he had won entitled him to respect.

Black Eagle swallowed and stared at the ground.

'The unbroken horse needs patience,' said the chief evenly. 'Yet once he has learned to ride as the others do he makes a fine mount. Tell me of your capture, Black Eagle.'

'I was hunting with two others,' said the young man. 'We found sign of a wagon and we followed it. Three men were in the wagon and they shot at us as we came close. One died.' He did not mention the name of the dead man, to do so would be against custom for the Indians believed that to mention a dead man by name was to call him back from the afterworld.

'One died,' said Painted Horse. 'Has the Shaman called his name for the last time and made him ready for the last journey?'

'This has been done.'

'It is well. Continue.'

'I shot my bow at the wagon and one of the white men fell. The other warrior and I rode close and yet another white man died. The last one I hit with the flat of my tomahawk and stunned. I brought him and his wagon to the village.'

'For torture?'

'The one who died was my friend. We were initiated together. He died bravely and I would see if the white man can die as well.'

'And the other warrior?'

'Was wounded and lies in his wigwam.' Black Eagle lifted his head and stared at the stern face of the chief. 'The white man dies.'

'I would speak with him.'

'He dies.'

'It shall be as Painted Horse decides,' said Red Dog sharply. 'Lead us to the white man.'

The prisoner was a thin, scrawny man with a bearded chin and a blood-stained bandage wound around his head. He was terrified, the Indians could almost smell his fear, and he crouched back in the wigwam, his hands held out as though to ward off a blow.

'You got me wrong!' he whined. 'I didn't mean no harm and I didn't fire no shots. It was them other fellas who started it all. I'm a friend of the Indians. I am. Traded with them years ago and lived with them for a time.' He swallowed, his Adam's apple bobbing in his throat, and switched to painful

Comanche. 'Friend,' he said and made the peace sign. 'Good friend.'

'Why did you come into our lands?' Painted Horse spoke in passable English. 'Were you not told that to do so would mean death?'

'No one told me nothing,' babbled the man. 'I was just riding to the hills with some supplies when those warriors jumped me.'

'You fired on them first.'

'Not me. The others did but not me.'

'Are not all white men as brothers?'

'They was strangers,' babbled the man. 'I was just giving them a ride out to the diggings.' He swallowed again. 'Look,' he pleaded. 'I ain't done no wrong to no Indian. I traded with them once and we got on fine. I'm your friend.' He repeated the word in the Indian gutturals. 'Friend. Smoke peace pipe, savvy?'

'He dies,' cried Black Eagle suddenly. He stepped towards the cringing man. 'He dies at the stake the death of fire.'

'No!' The trader recoiled, not under-standing the words but guessing from the tone just what the young warrior had said. 'You can't kill me.'

'Why not?' Painted Horse gestured the young warrior away from the prisoner. 'Why can we not kill you?'

'Because I'm your friend.' The prisoner paused and looked about the wigwam. His fear was passing, he had reached the bottom of terror and, like the rodent he was, his cunning was at work to find a way to save his skin. Lies meant nothing to him if he could get out of trouble. He would cheerfully burn the entire village in order to escape. He began speaking slowly and carefully.

'My name's Chigger, Hank Chigger, all the miners and a lot of Indians know me. I'm a trader, swapping goods for gold and furs.' He winked. 'You know the stuff, tobacco, fire-water, beads, bullets, rifles, all manner of things. You know what a trader is.'

'We know.' Painted Horse remained impassive.

'Well now.' Chigger had regained some of his shrewdness. 'I figure that I can be of more use to you alive than dead. There are things you must need, lots of things. Knives, cooking pots, ammunition, stuff like that. With the way things are you can't get them aside from raiding houses and settlements and that means that a lot of you get killed. I was thinking that maybe we could work a trade. You tell me what you want and I'll get it for you.' He extended his hands. 'Honest.'

For a long moment Painted Horse stared down at the man, then, abruptly, he turned and left the wigwam. The others followed him, Black Eagle last. The chief stared at him.

'By custom this prisoner is yours to do with as you will,' he said. 'No man can take that right from you. But you may give the prisoner to whom you wish. I will offer you three horses for him.'

'The price of a squaw,' said Red Dog and his hand gripped the arm of his son. 'Take it, Black Eagle. Laughing Moonlight, the daughter of Grey Owl has looked on you with eyes of softness. For three horses Grey Owl will sell her to you. I will arrange it.'

Black Eagle hesitated. He had sworn on oath that his friend would be avenged and he meant to keep that oath. But he too had looked on Laughing Moonlight with eyes of softness and longed for her to be his squaw. Three horses was wealth indeed, the only wealth the Indians recognized. Grey Owl was old and impatient and would take the gift of any young warrior. Unless he moved fast he could be too late.

But an oath was an oath. He said so.

'Did you swear to Manitou that this white man would die?' The Shaman, Bent Twig, the medicine man of the tribe had joined the group. He was old, withered, wise in the ways of men. He had been medicine man for a long time and could remember when white men were strange and greeted as messengers from the after-world. That had been a long time ago now, when men still used the cumbersome flintlocks and the Long Knives had not built their forts, the traders came with their firewater and the Indian still owned the prairies, fighting between themselves and collecting coup as they had done for many centuries.

'I swore.'

'To kill this particular man or to be avenged?' Bent Twig pressed the point.

'To be avenged,' admitted Black Eagle.

'It is well.' Bent Twig nodded as if verifying a decision. 'To break an oath is bad and must not be, but to sell this man would not be to break your oath. There are other white men.'

'Too many white men,' growled a warrior. 'They are as many as the buffalo.'

'To kill one buffalo and so frighten the herd is not wise,' said Painted Horse. 'Better to wait until all is ready and to kill them all at a blow.' He looked at the young warrior, his eyes glistening in the starlight. 'You will take the three horses?'

'Take them and I will see Grey Owl in the morning,' urged Red Dog. 'Is not Laughing Moonlight worth the scalp of a white man?'

'I will take the horses,' said Black Eagle suddenly. He looked at the Shaman. 'Is this shame?'

'It is wisdom, not shame,' said the medicine man. 'A true warrior does not merely count his coup, he thinks of the tribe as a whole. You have done well, Black Eagle, and Laughing Moonlight will thank you.'

'Go now,' said Painted Horse. 'Speak to Laughing Moonlight and tell her the words of heart-warming. Tomorrow she shall join you in your wigwam.' He sighed as he watched the young warrior move off between the wigwams, the light of the central fire touching his lithe body with copper luminescence.

'Three horses,' said Bent Twig. 'Many horses for one scalp.'

'Too many,' agreed the chief. 'And yet we need more than horses in the tribe. We need children, many children. It is better for me to lose horses than for Black Eagle to die without having taken a squaw.' He moved from the wigwam, past the guards squatting outside the hide structure.

'Where are the goods taken with the prisoner?'

Bent Twig led the way to the edge of the village.

5

The wagon was a rough, crude, high-bodied, big-wheeled structure common along the frontier. Drawn by a six-mule team it would cross rugged terrain and carry a surprising amount of freight. The mules had been unharnessed and cropped grass to one side of the village. A couple of Indian boys stood watch over them, breaking the monotony of their guardianship with play. The play, as all Indian play, was designed to build muscles and speed reflexes and they fought with twigs for knives, wrestled or held impromptu races. Painted Horse ignored them as he walked towards the wagon.

The body held an assortment of bales and containers. On the cargo was piled the weapons taken from the white men, long barrelled Colts of the latest pattern, using rimfire cartridges instead of the previous individual loads which needed percussion caps and were slow to reload. They rested in their holsters, the wide belts studded with the bright ammunition, together with the wickedly curved bowie knives, almost standard weapons on the frontier.

Painted Horse lifted out one of the pistols, examined it, dropped it back into its leather. Like all Indians he did not care for hand-guns, lacking the training necessary to become a good shot. Rifles were something else, they could be easily carried while in the saddle, easily aimed and, for the Indians, far better weapons than the heavy pistols with their relatively short ranges and demanded skill for useful operation. His eyes widened as he picked up an unfamiliar gun.

'Different,' said Red Dog. He picked up another. 'Much different. How do they work?'

He examined the weapon, touching the long tube beneath the barrel and the curved lever surrounding the trigger. His experience had been confined to the simple carbines such as the Spencer and Hawken, Sharps and Winslow, all breech-loading single-shot affairs. Slowly he operated the lever, grunting as a gleaming cartridge fell to the ground. Shutting the lever he saw that the hammer was at full cock and, without thinking, he pressed the trigger.

It was luck that no one was killed. Fire and smoke jetted from the muzzle and lead whined off into the night. Bent Twig, who had almost felt the wind of the passing bullet, jumped, his hand darting to his knife. Painted Horse, angry at the sudden shot, snatched the rifle from Red Dog.

'Does a warrior handle a gun like a stick? Do not enough Indians die beneath the guns of the white man that we must add to their number?'

'Wait.' Red Dog was too startled to take offence. 'I unloaded the weapon.'

'By firing it?'

'Before that.' Red Dog snatched the rifle and gripped the lever. 'See, I went like this and . . . ' His words died as another brass cartridge fell to the ground. Dazed, he operated the lever again, again, a third time and each time he did did so, another cartridge was expelled from the weapon.

'Let me see that.' Painted Horse snatched the rifle and operated the lever until the weapon was empty. Impatiently he tried to thrust the expelled cartridges back into the weapon, failed, then stood staring, thoughtfully down at the rifle.

'We have guns that fire one bullet and then have to be reloaded,' he said slowly. 'The Long Knives have rifles just like ours. Their pistols fire many times but their rifles but once.' He hefted the weapon. 'This gun holds many bullets. A warrior with such a weapon would be as many warriors. One brave could fire and fire and fire many bullets at our enemies.' He looked at the others. 'If Comanche had many such guns then they would be feared by all. It would be as though the dead had

85

come back to fight beside us.'

'Such guns would need many bullets,' said the Shaman wisely.

'We can get the bullets.'

'It would take many furs and hides to buy the bullets.'

'With more of these guns we can kill more game.'

'Our young warriors are not as they were,' said the Shaman. 'Once, when I was young, a brave could fire an arrow and then a second arrow and then a third and all would be in the air at one time. He could take his bow and shoot an arrow beyond the sight of man and then a second and when they were examined the second would have split the first. They have forgotten how to do that now.'

'They can still shoot fast and far.'

'Now they use the guns of the white man. Such guns a child may use for they need only the strength of a finger.'

'What are you saying Bent Twig?' Painted Arrow respected the wisdom of the medicine man. 'Speak with a straight tongue.'

'If a man has many bullets in his gun he will not worry to send the first one to the target. He will hope to shoot three bullets instead of one. He will be as a man with many arrows on his bow string, many can so be fired at one time, none will hit where he hopes. And these guns will need many bullets. Game is scarce now and the buffalo will not last for ever. Where will come the furs and hides to buy all the bullets these guns will need?'

'You speak like an old woman, Shaman,' said Red Dog rudely. 'Does a warrior carry but one arrow in his quiver? Does he shoot them all because he carries many?'

'An arrow can be made in a wigwam during the winter,' said the Shaman. 'It will kill and can be used many times. Bullets can be used but once.'

'White men do not fight with arrows,' snapped Painted Horse. He stooped, picked up the cartridges and, taking the rifle led the way back to where the prisoner waited in the wigwam.

He looked up as the Indians entered, his eyes widening at the sight of the rifle.

'So you found them,' he said. 'Good, eh, Chief?'

'What are they?' Painted Horse held out the rifle. 'Show me how they work.' He held out the cartridges.

'The Winchester? Sure.' Chigger knew better than to be clever. With the loaded rifle he could kill many Indians but not all. His death, should he try to fight his way out, would be something special in the way of Indian ingenuity. He loaded, ejected the shells and reloaded the magazine. He did it several times until the Indians knew exectly how to do it. Painted Horse took the loaded rifle, handed it to Red Dog and sat facing the prisoner.

'What goods does your wagon contain?'

'Goods?' Chigger looked blank. 'Didn't you look?'

'I asked a question, you will answer.'

'Sure.' The trader shrugged. 'Whiskey, ammunition, some blasting powder and pick heads. I was going to the mines,' he explained. 'The diggers can always use whiskey.'

'Firewater.' Painted Horse turned to Red Dog. 'Go to the wagon and remove all it contains. Take the bullets and powder and anything that may be of use. The fire-water you will throw to the ground. Is this understood?'

The warrior nodded and slipped away.

'You are a white man,' said Painted Horse slowly. 'You killed one of my warriors and for this you deserve to die.' His voice thickened. 'There are many ways for a man to die. He can die quick as in battle or he can die slow as a man tormented by the evil spirits. He can die bravely or he can die as a woman.' He stared at the trader. 'It comes to me that you do not know how to die. It would be pleasant to see how long you can remain silent beneath the knives of our squaws.'

'You ain't going to kill me!' Chigger trembled to a return of his fears.

'Each man dies when his time is due,' said the chief. 'It may be that your time has come. And yet I will be merciful to you and let you choose the manner of your passing. Death by fire at the stake. Death by torture. Death by running the gauntlet. Choose.'

'You ain't serious?' Chigger swallowed. He knew of the Indians' peculiar sense of humour and knew, unlike most people living east, that their sense of humour was a strong one. They would laugh at simple things but they would laugh even stronger at something which incurred physical discomfort or pain.

'You think I joke?' Painted Horse made a sign to the Shaman. Bent Twig stepped behind the trader and whipped a loop of rawhide about his forehead. He adjusted it until it rested just above the eyes. Slipping a stick in the loop he twisted until the thong dug into the flesh. Chigger screamed, fell silent, screamed again as the Shaman tightened the thong.

'He is a woman,' grunted a watching warrior. 'He cries at the thought of death.'

'He cries as a squaw cries when she has lost her son,' said another. 'He will provide little sport.'

'He will amuse the children,' said Painted Horse, carelessly. At his signal the Shaman tightened the thong still further.

'No!' screamed the trader. 'You're busting my head. No!'

'Enough!' Painted Horse stared at the trembling white man as the Shaman removed the thong. Around the trader's forehead ran a red weal. The thong had not really been applied tightly. Chigger's fear at what would happen if the Shaman had really twisted it tight had hurt him more than the actual physical pain. He rubbed at the weal and stared with wild eyes about the wigwam.

'Choose.' Painted Horse stared at the trader.

'I'll run the gauntlet,' said Chigger. 'But you got to play fair.'

Running the gauntlet was the only punishment where the victim stood a chance of life. He was stripped to the waist, the warriors, children and women of the village lined up in a double column facing each other and each held a weapon of some blunt nature. The victim had to run between the lines and, as he did so, all within reach beat, clawed and struck at his body. A hard man, fast, quick on his feet and physically strong could, if he were lucky, reach the waiting horse at the end of the double line. Once he reached it he was allowed to escape.

'A coward's choice,' grumbled a warrior. 'A man would have chosen to die by torment.'

Painted Horse made no comment. Had Chigger chosen such a death he would have been respected by the Indians, who, above all, valued personal valour and courage. His choice had, in their eyes, branded him as an abject coward. But Painted Horse did not intend that Chigger should die.

'You value your life,' he said. 'Is that not so?'

'Who don't?' Chigger ceased rubbing at his head. 'You going to kill me?'

'If you fail us, yes.' The chief picked up the Winchester. 'If I let you go will you return with many guns like this and with many bullets for the guns?'

'What?' The trader stared in amazement, then, as the shrewd mind grasped what was behind the chief's words, he almost fainted in relief. The torture, the talk of death, the grim faces had all been to scare him. Now he was being offered his life for a promise. The fact that the Indians expected him to keep his promise did not bother him in the slightest. 'You want rifles, is that it?'

'Yes.'

'I can get you guns,' said the trader. 'Lots of them.'

'Like this one?'

'Repeating rifles are scarce,' said Chigger. 'Not too many of them in this part of the country yet. I'd have to send east for them and they come dear.' He spoke in Comanche. 'Many furs, Many hides.'

'You get us guns or you die.'

'Be reasonable,' said Chigger. He appealed to the chief. 'Look, I could make a promise and forget it as soon as I'm out of sight. But I don't act that way. If you want to make a deal then that's all right by me. But guns cost money, gold understand? I've got to pay for them cash on the nail. I haven't got money so I can't buy them.' He spread his hands. 'Sorry, Chief, but that's how it is. I want to help you but I can't do the impossible.'

Painted Horse had listened to his words with enigmatic eyes. He spoke, his hands caressing the walnut stock of the rifle.

'You speak with a forked tongue, white man, and this I know. But also I know that, in one thing, you have spoken straight words. I have been to your stores and have seen the way you trade. You pay gold for the things you need. How much of the yellow stone would one rifle need?'

'A hundred dollars,' said Chigger immediately. His own rifle had cost fifty. Not that it mattered, Indians had no idea of the purchasing power of money or gold. To them gold was merely a yellow stone and they could never understand why the white men wanted it so much. It was an attitude of mind that left them wide open to cheating traders.

'Much gold.' Painted Horse nodded. He did not trust the trader and, had the man made wild promises, he would have killed him with his own hands. And yet he wanted the new repeating rifles and wanted them badly. Chigger could get them for him, of that there was no doubt; but, as Chigger had said, rifles required gold to buy them.

'You give me gold,' said Chigger eagerly. 'As much gold as you can get and I'll go and buy you the rifles. I'll need my wagon, of course, and mules, and you'd best give me my weapons, I don't want to be robbed. I'll head east to the railhead, see the agent, have the guns and ammunition shipped, freight them out here to you and everyone will be happy.' He did not add that he would be the happiest of all. He had no compunction at selling guns to the Indians or trading with the men who had killed his companions. All he wanted to do was to get away from here with a whole skin.

'I will give you the gold,' said Painted Horse abruptly. 'Much gold for many guns and the bullets for the guns.'

'You will?' Chigger almost rubbed his hands. 'Good. That's fine.'

'He will cheat you,' said the Shaman. 'He will take the yellow stone and he will not return.'

'That is in his mind,' agreed Painted Horse.

'Then why trust him?'

'I trust him because I must. Our warriors need the rifles which speak many times. With them we can fight off

96

our enemies and kill the Long Knives.'

'He will cheat you.' The Shaman folded his arms. 'I have spoken.'

'I am not a new-blooded warrior,' said Painted Horse. 'I am not a babe to be cheated by the moon into thinking the world is made of whiteness. Nor am I touched by Manitou so that I seek to talk to myself in a quiet pool.'

'You are not touched by Manitou,' agreed the Shaman. Insanity was so rare among the Indians that any mentally derranged unfortunate was said to have been touched by Manitou and considered almost sacred. Such a one was fed and clothed and not expected to do any of the work around the village.

'And I will not be cheated.' Painted Horse looked at the white man. 'My eyes seek your heart,' he said. 'Your heart is black and your tongue speaks not the truth. You think that you will take our gold and leave us with your promises. Do I speak with a straight tongue?'

He did but Chigger dared not admit it. He swallowed, spread his hands, smiled and protested good intentions. The fact that he was perfectly willing to sell rifles which would be used against his own people did not bother him.

'I will give you gold,' said Painted Horse. 'You will bring us the guns and many bullets. When you return we shall give you twice as much gold as before. You will then buy more guns and more bullets. Each time you return you shall have twice as much of the yellow stone.'

'You mean it?' Chigger's eyes almost started from his head at the thought of the profits he would be making. Allowing for setting his own value on the guns in the first place the promise of double gold on his return seemed almost too good to be true. And the Indian promised to double up each time. A few such trips and the trader would be a rich man.

'An Indian does not lie,' said Painted Horse sternly.

'I know.' Chigger did know, an

Indian's word was never broken. 'But what you promise will take a hell of a lot of gold. Have you got it?'

'I do not speak empty words.'

'Sure, but you Indians don't go in for mining.' Chigger's eyes gleamed at a sudden thought. 'There's a big lode around here, is that it? A place where you just pick the pay dirt up in nuggets.'

'We do not collect the yellow stone,' said the chief coldly. 'Such work is for children and fools of white men. But you shall have the gold. The second dawn from now you shall have it. Tomorrow you will teach my young men and my warriors how to use the gun which shoots many times.' He rose, tall and proud in his beaded tunic. 'And forget not this. Fail us and you die the death you have chosen. I have spoken.'

He left the trader alone with his thoughts.

6

Bill Underwood was a desert rat, a sun-toughened old man who had spent his life grubbing in the stony wilderness of the Blanca Hills in search of the elusive El Dorado which was every prospector's dream. He shared his diggings with Jud, another old timer whose last name no one knew. Together they tore down the rock, panned the streams and, slowly accumulated a poke of the precious metal. It was hard work, long tedious labour with no company but that of themselves and their mules, but neither man would have had it any other way.

Bill stepped to the door of the flimsy cabin and yelled down the gulley towards his invisible partner. 'Hey, Jud, come and get it.'

'What we got?' Jud wiped his hands on his jeans, wiped his face with a bandanna and climbed towards the cabin. 'Beans? Beans and bacon? Bacon? Or did you get a rabbit like you promised?'

'No rabbit.' Bill led the way inside the cabin. 'Just beans and coffee.' He served up the meal. 'That trader fella. What's his name?'

'Chigger.'

'That's right. That Chigger didn't show up like he said he would, and we're plumb out of grub and whiskey.'

Bill wiped his plate with the last of the hard tack, and buried his face in his coffee mug.

'Maybe you could get something to eat off the others?' Jud scowled down at his tin plate. 'There's the Broncho twins over at the Stardust mines and old man Harrison with his three sons at the Go-Ahead diggings. I don't reckon they'd see us starve.'

'If Chigger ain't been around then they'd be as short as we are.' Bill picked at his teeth with the point of his knife. 'Reckon I'll go out tomorrow and see what I can shoot.'

'Hunting don't pay when there's gold to be collected,' reminded Jud. 'If we're partners then I don't aim to do all the work.'

'You can't see the foresight of a rifle your eyes are so bad,' said Bill. 'Better leave it to me.'

'We could ride down to the fort,' said his partner. 'Couple of days and we'd be there. I reckon the colonel would fit us out.'

'Maybe.'

'Austin's a good man.'

'I know it.' Bill returned the knife to its sheath. 'But he's got the notion the Indians are out scalp hunting again. He wanted to clear the hills and get us to stay inside the fort. He said we'd be safer there.'

'He's right,' agreed Jud. He looked at his partner. 'When did you learn all this?'

'Harrison's youngest told me. He went down to pick up some cartridges and the colonel sent word by him that all prospectors should quit their claims and get to the fort. The boy said the colonel only let him go because his Pa was waiting for him.'

'Indian trouble.' Jud shivered and stared outside to where the setting sun threw long shadows over the hills. 'Gold ain't worth losing your scalp for, Bill.'

'Did I say it was?'

'No, but I know you. You get gold fever and the devil himself couldn't frighten you from a claim.' The old man stared from his weak eyes. 'What you aim to do, Bill?'

'Indians don't scare me,' said the prospector. 'I've fought them before and I will again I guess, but that's not all there is to it. We've got a nice little claim here and we're piling up the dust. If we quit now then jumpers may grab it. If we stay to work it then we need food.' He burped. 'Them beans is getting a mite wearisome day after day. And no whiskey either.'

'We can live without whiskey.'

'Not if a rattler gets you.' Bill looked

thoughtfully at the approaching night. 'If we go down to the fort the colonel will grab us. If we stay here we starve unless I can get us some game. It's a problem, Jud.'

'How bad are the Indians?'

'Same as usual, I guess. I ain't heard no drums or seen no smoke. Sure, if a war party catches us they may try to take our hair, but that ain't new.' He slapped the holster at his side. 'Anyways, I can always fight them off.'

'You can? What about me?'

'With your eyes you couldn't tell an Indian in full paint from a cavalry man in dress uniform,' chuckled Bill. 'The next time you hit town you ain't going to get a drink until the eye-man fits you up with them spectacle things. Then maybe you'll be able to tell night from day.'

'I can tell a nugget from a stone anyways.' Jud was short sighted but at close range his vision was good. The trouble was that the range was very close, normally he panned his gold about six inches from his eyes. A pistol or rifle was something he just couldn't see to use and so carried neither.

Bill busied himself washing the few dishes with a little water, scrubbing them with sand and stacking them away. He took a canvas sack from his pocket, spilled the last few grains of tobacco it held into a scrap of paper, twisted it and lit it from the fire. He took three puffs, saw that Jud wasn't smoking, and handed the crude cigarette to his partner.

'Finish it Jud.'

'Thanks.' The old man smoked in silence, his brow furrowed with thought. 'Bill?'

'Yes?'

'That was the last of your tobacco, wasn't it?'

'Yes.'

'We've hit the bottom then ain't we, Bill?'

'We're out of grub and tobacco and whiskey,' admitted the prospector. 'But we've got plenty of dust.' He stooped, lifted a loose board and lifted out a pair of heavy canvas sacks. He put them on the table, the precious metal they contained making a dull thud as it hit the boards. 'Enough dust and nuggets to buy us all the food and whiskey we could use,' he said.

'You can't eat gold,' said Jud. He rubbed his stubbled chin. 'Bill, I've been thinking.'

'You have?'

'Sure. With my eyes the way they are I'm not much good. I can heft a pick and pan a stream all right, but if trouble comes then I'm just in the way.'

'Who says so?' Bill was quick to the defence of his partner.

'I say so,' said Jud. 'So I've got an idea. How about us going down to the fort, stacking up with grub, then heading for the town so I can get me fitted up with eyewindows? That way I'd be able to carry a gun again and beat off the Indians should they be after my hair.' He looked at his hands. 'It ain't that I'm scared, Bill,' he said quietly. 'But it ain't comfortable to know that you might be leaning against an Indian thinking that it's a rock.'

'You getting that bad. Jud?' Bill had known about his partner's short sight but he had not thought that it was as bad as it was. Jud nodded.

'Guess it must be the sun,' he said. 'It's getting so that I'm shaving by memory.' He touched his chin. 'And my memory ain't that good.'

It was a joke, but it was serious all the same. A man in Indian Territory needed his wits and weapons about him at all times. A man could carry his partner just so far but, if the worst came to the worst, then a friend who could not see to fire a gun was a liability. Bill rubbed his chin.

'We'll do it.' he said. 'Tell you what we'll do. Chigger ain't coming now and we can't hope for grub from him. The fort's two days' ride away and we're out of beans. If the Indians are out then we don't want to go shooting off the rifle. I'll ride over to the Harrisons tonight, they ain't too far, and see if I can borrow some food. I'll find out what the news is, pass the word that we're pulling out and see if they'll keep an eye on our claim.' He stretched. 'Might even borrow some tobacco. With the moon coming up I should be back well before dawn and we can start right out. You be all right on your own?'

'You leave me the rifle?'

'Yes, loaded and ready. I'll whistle the usual tune when I come back so don't shoot me thinking I'm an Indian. If anyone else comes you give them one chance and then let go. The noise may scare them even if you miss.'

It was dark when Bill started out. Before leaving he checked the rifle and the pistol he carried at his waist. It was one of the old Frontier Colts, each chamber being loaded with powder, wad and ball, the whole rammed home tight with the built-in rammer. He checked each load, placed fresh caps on the nipples and put some extra charges in his pockets. Filling his canteen he mounted his mule and went jogging over the mountains towards the Harrison diggings.

It was very quiet and the sounds of his mule's hooves as the agile beast found footholds on the stony ground echoed from the surrounding hills. After a while the moon rose, throwing a pale light over the terrain and, in the pale luminescence, the hills had a hard, bone-white bleached look as if he were riding through a valley of the dead.

Bill was not imaginative, he had lived too long on his own to be afraid of tricks of lighting and the effects of shadow. But he wished that he had tobacco so that he could smoke and he wished that the Indians were not a newly aroused menace. He found himself staring over his shoulder and twice, at an imagined sound, he twisted in the saddle, the heavy Colt in his hand, one thumb levering back the hammer.

Harrison's diggings lay across the range, a jumbled place of ledges and gullies from which the big miner and his three sons tore a modicum of gold. They had been there for two years now and, despite all Harrison's statements that he was going to surrender the claim and take up an easy life such as cattle raising or buffalo hunting he was still there.

Bill slowed as he approached the diggings, knowing that strangers were not welcome in the goldfields unless expected. He reined in his mule and called down to the shadowy bulk of the cabin he could just make out in the light of the moon.

'Harrison! Hey, Harrison! It's me, Bill Underwood.'

Silence.

He called again, a third time and then, feeling a sudden chill, dug his heels into the side of the mule and forced it downwards along the winding path to the cabin.

He called again when a few yards away.

'Anyone awake? It's me, Harrison.

Bill from across the range. Ain't I welcome?'

The rolling echoes sent back his voice distorted and jumbled so that a legion of ghosts seemed to be wailing in the night. The cabin remained dark and silent.

Bill halted and wiped his forehead. The Harrisons could have pulled out without letting him know, it was possible but unlikely. Or they could all be asleep, again possible but very unlikely. They were aware of the Indian menace and surely would have left one of their number on guard. Slipping from the saddle Bill drew his pistol, cocked it, and, with it levelled in his hand, stepped towards the cabin.

The Harrisons were still there. He opened the door and something heavy yielded as he pressed. Inside was darkness, darker from the moonlight outside. Bill hesitated, his nostrils twitching, then taking a match from his pocket struck it and stared about in the light of the tiny torch.

A man stared at him with wide, empty eyes. Another rested in a corner, something long and slender sprouting from his chest. A third seemed to grin from an impossible position. The match burned low and burned his fingers. Bill swore, struck another, found a lamp, ignited the wick and settled the chimney with a shaking hand.

'Dead,' Bill muttered. 'All dead.'

The man who had stared at him was old man Harrison himself. At first glance Bill thought that he had been scalped, then remembered the man's baldness and saw that the red stains on his head surrounded the gap of a tomahawk wound. His eldest son had lost his hair, his throat was cut and he had two bullet holes in the body. The youngest was the one with the arrow sticking from his chest and the third son had slumped against the door. All three of the boys had been scalped, a neat circle of skin and hair torn from the crowns of their heads.

'Dead,' said Bill again. He sniffed at

the air in the cabin. There was a faint trace of burnt powder, the stench of blood and, faintly, the tell-tale smell of the grease with which the Indians rubbed themselves. He stooped over the bodies and then examined the interior of the cabin. There were no weapons, no food, no blankets or knives. He looked into cupboards and found them stripped of everything of value to an Indian. Even the tobacco and whiskey he knew were kept on the second shelf had gone.

He straightened and stared about the cabin, sensing something wrong but not knowing just what it was. Boards had been ripped from one corner of the cabin floor. Bill stooped over the opening exposed, touched the rough wood with his finger and then looked at his skin in the light of the lamp. Minute traces of yellow metal shone in the soft light.

'They found his cache.' He stared around, puzzled. The arrow, tomahawk wound and scalping told of Indians.

The theft of the gold did not. Indians did not value gold and would not have burdened themselves with it. On the other hand Indians would have fired the cabin. The absence of any dead Indians meant nothing, the red warriors always removed their dead and wounded from a battle.

From somewhere outside an owl hooted, was answered from a far distance, then was repeated near at hand. Immediately Bill doused the light and stood breathing softly in the close darkness. The owl hooted again, something hummed in the night and the mule screamed and drummed its hooves.

'Hell!' The old prospector was no coward and he had an affection for his mule. He dropped low, ran through the cabin door and flung himself towards a patch of shadow close to where he had left the mule. It was empty and he rolled as he hit dirt. A few feet away the mule had fallen silent, a dark shadow on the edge of darkness. An arrow, its feathers dark in the moonlight, showed what had caused the scream and the drumming.

Even as Bill stared another arrow hummed towards him, plucking at his sleeve as it shattered against the rocks behind.

'Jud!' Bill wet his lips as he thought of his almost blind partner alone in the cabin. The Indians were on the warpath, there could no longer be any doubt. They had struck at the Harrisons just before sunset, wiping out the four men in one unexpected charge. A few had remained, perhaps those who had searched for the gold and Bill had arrived just after they had left. Now they were amusing themselves using him as a target for their arrows.

For a long moment Bill waited in the darkness, the Colt heavy in his hand. Another arrow whispered towards him, brushing so close in that the feathers rasped his cheek and, as it did so, he screamed and collapsed to the ground.

Lying there, the Colt ready and

cocked in his hand, he waited.

He waited as the moon moved across the sky and the shadows lengthened about him. He waited with screaming nerves expecting another arrow, better aimed, to thrust its way into his yielding flesh. He waited until his eyes burned beneath their lowered lids and his hands felt cold and numb. And then he saw the Indian.

He came like a ghost, like a painted devil straight from hell, his face grotesque and disfigured by the paint on his face and body. He stood for a long moment on the edge of the moonlight, his eyes glistening a little from the reflected light, his tomahawk in his hand as he poised himself for the final leaping rush, the skull-cracking blow and then the swift slicing with the scalping knife at his belt.

Bill did not move. He lay, his eyes slitted so as not to betray him by their white glisten in the moonlight, holding his breath so as to make no sound. The Indian could be alone, a solitary scout after an easy scalp, or he could be one of a watching and waiting party. The prospector did not know and could not tell. All he knew was that the red devil was poising himself, tomahawk swinging high, leg muscles bunching as he made ready to leap on the prostrate man.

The hand holding the Colt moved, the trigger finger tightened and thunder and flame stabbed from ground level towards the charging Indian. Even as the echoes of the shot rolled from the hills Bill was scrambling to his feet, the gun levelled for a second shot. It was not necessary. The Indian, an ounce of lead driven between the eyes and blood washing the pain from his face, twitched and jerked in his death throes on the stony ground.

One look Bill gave him and then was away, his legs thrusting at rock and stone as he flung himself into deeper shadow. Upwards he climbed, the skin between his shoulder blades twitching as he anticipated the shocking impact of an arrow. Higher he climbed, higher, heading as fast as his old legs could carry him across the range and back to the lone man he had left waiting his return.

Dawn found him footsore and weary still two miles from the cabin. He had taken short cuts, risking his life in the mountains until, in the darkness before dawn, he had been forced to rest. He had forced himself to sit and take great gulps of air, to rest his aching head against the cold stone and to wait until his quivering nerves and pounding heart had settled so as to allow him to continue the journey.

He heard the sound of the rifle while still a mile from the cabin.

It echoed thin and distant like the muffled sound of a whip. It faded even as he tensed and strained his cars but no other shots came and, after a moment, he continued his sliding progress. As he came in sight of the cabin caution made him halt and take stock.

The gulley was deserted. Jud's mule stood in its corral, head lifted and eyes wild. An Indian, bow bent, was about to drive an arrow into the beast, taking his time about it and seeming to enjoy himself. Bill raised his Colt then lowered it as he recognized the extreme range. A shot now would only attract attention and would serve no purpose. He swore as the bow hummed and the arrow, moving like a flash, thudded into the mule. The beast fell like a pole-axed steer, the long shaft penetrating the heart. The Indian laughed, called something over his shoulder and walked towards his waiting pony. Bill, crouching behind a rock, watched the warrior mount, turn the head of the horse, and gallop away.

Jud was dead. It was no surprise, the prospector had expected nothing else. The old, almost blind man lay in a pool of his own blood beside a gaping opening in the floor. Jud was dead and the gold was gone.

Anger blinded the old prospector to

his own danger. He ran from the cabin and clawed his way up the steep rocks behind the shanty. At the top he wriggled over the skyline and stared down at the trail below. He had been quick and he had beaten the Indians. They came riding past in single file, their paint red and yellow, green and brown in the full light of the morning sun. Bill waited until they had passed, slithered down the rocks and, as he jumped on the trail, lifted the Colt and opened fire.

He had five shots left in the weapon and he used them all. Two warriors threw up their hands and toppled from their horses. The third, a red streak appearing on his side, yelled and threw himself from his mount. The others, six painted warriors, galloped down the trail looking for cover.

Bill jumped from the trail, scrambled up a rocky slope, found a niche and wedged himself into it. From his pocket he took the spare charges for his gun and, ripping them open with his teeth, poured the measured charge of powder into the chambers of his revolver, thrust in the case containing the ball and rammed it home with the rammer beneath the long barrel. With trembling fingers he fitted percussion caps on the nipples and then, the Colt fully loaded, settled down to take as many Indians with him into death as possible.

7

Major Perlis sat tiredly in his saddle and cursed the Confederate marksman who had crippled his leg. Back home the wound had not seemed a disadvantage, it had lent him a little glamour, a touch of romance so that people had clustered around him and called him brave and heroic to have risked his life for the Union cause. They had wanted to hear the story, which had lost nothing in the telling, and had fêted him during his leave.

But that was back home in civilization, back in Vermont where people did not walk with guns at their hips and a watchful expression in their eyes, where painted Indians provided no menace and food was eaten from linen-covered tables with silver and fine glass to turn each meal into a ceremony.

Here in the barren foothills of the

Blanca range the wound was nothing but a nuisance. It made him limp which he could bear but it also made his leg ache after a few hours in the saddle. Now, as he rode, he tried to rest the limb, wondering for the hundredth time whether it would be the path of wisdom to resign his commission and return home. Pride stopped him, that and the hope of a career. He was an officer and his country needed his services and, if he hoped for promotion and a high-ranking post then he had to sweat out his assignment here in this God-forsaken territory.

He reined in his mount as a thin sound echoed across the hills.

'Sergeant!'

'Sir!' Gilcross rode forward to the officer's side.

'Did you hear that?'

'Sounded like a shot to me.' The scarred man spat a stream of tobacco juice into the dust. 'Come from the north by the sound of it.'

'That's Underwood's diggings, isn't

it?' Major Perlis squinted around him, wishing that the terrain was not such a jumble of broken rock and dusty scrub. Even intensive map reading had not familiarized him with the locale and he guessed the source of the shot merely because they were heading towards the diggings.

'That's right.' Gilcross knew the area as well as he knew the lines on his face. He frowned as a second shot echoed from the distance. 'Better get up there, Major. Bill may be in trouble.'

Perlis nodded and spurred his mount forward. Behind him came the rest of the patrol, a dozen men including Terrance, Sweeny and four other volunteers. Gilcross automatically led the way, choosing little paths winding between jumbled stone, urging his mount forward at top speed.

As they advanced the sound of shots became louder, echoing spitefully around them and, after easing his mount along a narrow gulley, Gilcross led the way towards a rough cabin set against a wall.

He took one look at the arrow imbedded in the dead mule, a second into the interior of the cabin, then he had dismounted, his rifle in his hands.

'They're around the bend,' he reported. 'Indians for sure. You want me to take half the men over the hill and make a flank attack while you ride along the trail?'

It was good advice and Perlis knew it. The sergeant knew the conditions better than he did and was an old Indian fighter. He nodded, gesturing towards Terrance and five other men.

'Follow the sergeant,' he ordered. 'The rest of you come with me.' He rode on a swinging path intended to circle the area from where the firing had come. Gilcross, scrambling up the rock like an agile goat, led his party over the bluff and across the skyline. He dropped as they came into view of the trail.

'Pick your target,' he ordered. 'Fire on the word.' He squinted along the barrel of his Spencer carbine. 'Ready! Fire!'

Six shots sounded as one and a hail of lead whined down to where half-seen shapes crouched behind boulders, the smoke from the rifles lifting into the hot, morning air.

'Reload!' snapped the sergeant. 'Aim. Fire!'

An Indian screamed as he sprang from cover, a horrible redness marring his features. Another toppled forward, his feathered coup-stick flying from his hand. Then the Indians were running, copper shadows against the rock and scrub. Before the rifles could be reloaded they had vanished to the thudding of flying hooves.

'That's it.' Gilcross slung his rifle and slid down the rocks. 'Let's see what they were after.'

'What about the major?' Terrance joined the sergeant in his downward path. 'Shouldn't we let him know the Indians are routed?'

'He'll find out for himself.' Gilcross spat. 'He should have been in position by the time we opened fire.' He looked at Terrance. 'All right, so it's bad tactics. I should have waited until the major was in position then we'd have caught the Indians in a cross-fire. That's what it says in the book, isn't it?'

'Something like that,' admitted Terrance. He did not want to argue.

'The books on Indian fighting haven't been written,' said Gilcross. 'They knew we were here and they knew what we were after. Had we waited we wouldn't have got one of them and the major would maybe have lost a couple of men and horses. This is natural country to the Indians, they can move as soft as a lizard among these rocks. Anyway, there was someone who needed help and needed it fast. Tactics may have got a couple more Indians but it may have got him an Indian haircut.' The sergeant halted beside a niche in the stone. 'You all right in there?'

'I'm alive.' Bill Underwood looked up at the weathered and scarred cheek. He tried to grin. 'So it's you, Gil, might have guessed it.'

'Me and the army.' The sergeant stooped beside the old prospector. 'Where did they get you, Bill?'

'Couple of places.' Bill winced as the sergeant slipped his hand under his arms and pulled him into the open. 'Ricochet I think and one of them feathered stickers got me in the back.' He swallowed. 'They got Jud.'

'I saw him.' Steel flashed in the sunlight as the sergeant cut away the blood-soaked clothing. He turned to the white-faced recruits standing by the watchful Terrance. 'Go get the horses and bring them here. Get me a canteen. Move!'

'Can I help?' Terrance joined the sergeant, kneeling beside the prospector. Gilcross grunted.

'Know any doctoring?'

'A little.' Terrance pursed his lips as he examined the wounds. One of them, an ugly hole in the right thigh, had been made by a ricocheting bullet. With the point of his knife Terrance jerked out the shapeless bullet, his hands moving so fast that the crude operation was over before the prospector had guessed what he was about to do.

'Wash and bind that wound,' ordered the captain. 'The ball missed the artery so he won't lose much blood. You got any whiskey?'

'Whiskey?' Gilcross looked blank. 'Where would I be getting whiskey from?'

'From that canteen of yours.' Terrance stared him in the eye. 'Got any?'

'Yes,' admitted Gilcross sullenly.

'Get it. Wash the wound with it after you've used water and before you bind it up. It'll stop infection.' He looked down the trail. 'Where the hell are the men you sent for the horses?'

They arrived at that moment, the iron shoes on the horses clattering on the ground. Gilcross yelled quick orders and then his voice changed as Perlis came into view. Terrance heard him give his report as he tended the wounded man.

The arrow was imbedded deep in the muscles of the back just below the left shoulder. A little lower and it would have penetrated the heart, higher and it would have splintered bone. Terrance examined it, probing around the wickedly barbed head buried in the flesh. Bill sucked in his breath as pain tore through him then managed a weak grin.

'Did I hear you talk of whiskey?'

Major Perlis called before Terrance could answer and he rose, walked down to the trail and stared up at the officer.

'Sir?'

'The sergeant tells me that Underwood is badly hurt. Is that right?'

'Too hurt to move until something is done about that arrow in his back. If we move him the barbs will tear down into his lung. His only chance is to cut it out before he is shifted.'

'I see.' The major frowned as he stared into the distance. 'It appears that the Indians have raided this digging. My orders are to circulate all the claims and order the prospectors to join us and ride back to the fort.' He hesitated. 'Gilcross tells me that the next digging is the Harrison place, a few hours' ride from here. I don't like to leave Underwood without medical attention and yet, at the same time, he obviously can't ride with us. Have you any medical knowledge?'

'Yes, sir.'

'You can see my problem. Splitting my force will be to invite trouble. On the other hand the path back to the fort seems clear. If Underwood could be treated so as to be able to sit a horse he could be sent back while we press on.'

'I can treat Underwood,' said Terrance. 'Give me a couple of men to hold him down, the sergeant and Sweeny will do. Have the others make a horse-stretcher. We can ride him between two horses and he'll be as comfortable as we can make him.' He turned to Gilcross. 'You got those canteens?'

'I've got them.'

'Then let's get to work.'

Terrance led the way back to the injured man, doffed his tunic, rolled up his sleeves and slipped his knife from its sheath. It was, big, clumsy for such delicate work and he frowned at it. 'Sweeny, you have a smaller knife?'

'This one?' Sweeny held out the blade he had showed Terrance in the prison. It was small, razor sharp and with a needle point. Terrance nodded as he took it.

'Treat the leg first,' he ordered the sergeant. 'Do as I told you.' He smiled down at the sweating face of the prospector. 'This is going to hurt a mite, Bill,' he said. 'But it will soon be over and it will save your life. Anything you want to say before we start?'

'The Indians got the Harrisons,' said the old prospector. 'Got all of them and stole their gold. I went over to see them, found the bodies and came running back to Jud. I arrived too late.' He grunted as the sergeant bandaged his wounded thigh. 'Damn Indians! If I'd have had one of the Navy Colts like you carry I would have done for the lot of them. Takes too long to reload the cap and ball model I carry around. Good enough for most things but when a man needs plenty of fire-power he ain't got it.'

'You did all right,' said Terrance. 'Three dead from what I could see.'

'I was down to the last bullet but one,' gasped the prospector. 'I was saving that for myself. Comanches ain't what you'd call gentle with a man when they catch him and I'm too old to stand much of what they like to hand out.' He licked his lips. 'How about that whiskey?'

'Have a drink of water.'

'I'd rather have whiskey.'

'You can have whiskey later,' said Terrance. He lifted the canteen the sergeant handed him and shook it, listening to the swish of the contents. 'One swig,' he said. 'One drink and that's all.' He held the canteen to Bill's lips, tilted it and let some of the raw spirit trickle down the injured man's throat.

Withdrawing the canteen he nodded to Sweeny and Gilcross and, as they turned the old prospector on his face, washed his hands, the area around the wound and the blade of the small knife with the raw alcohol.

'Yell all you want,' he said to Bill. 'Yell, but don't move.'

Deliberately he began to cut out the arrow.

Bill heaved, a thick sound coming from his throat and the two men holding him fought to prevent him from twisting away. Terrance worked swiftly, the blade of the knife, now dulled with blood, cutting the torn flesh from around the arrow. To pull out the shaft was impossible, the barbs would do more damage coming out than they had going in and the resultant haemorrhage would have been swiftly fatal. And yet, so deep was the arrow, so near the lung, that it took skill to cut out the barbed head without doing more damage than could be helped.

Terrance grunted, gripped the shaft and pulled the arrow along the path he had cut for it. Bill yelled as pain stabbed through him and blood oozed from the open wound on his back. Terrance tossed aside the arrow, tilted a water canteen over the wound and followed it with a gush of whiskey. Bill shuddered, strained and then slumped into unconsciousness.

'He's dead,' said Sweeny.

'Fainted.' Terrance soaked up the blood in a scrap of fabric. With the point of his knife he teased a field dressing until the bandage was an open web of cotton strands, washed the wound again with whiskey and placed the mesh over the torn flesh. He soaked a second scrap of teased-out cotton over it and then a third, soaking them with still more alcohol.

'This will take up the blood and help it to clot and close the wound,' he explained. 'The rotgut will prevent infection.' He reached for more bandages from the emergency kit the sergeant had collected from his saddle-bags.

'Now we'll tie him up good and tight so he can't jerk his muscles and then wake him up.'

'Will he live?' Gilcross was anxious.

'Depends.'

'Depends on what?'

'On many things.' Terrance fastened the last bandage. 'On his constitution, whether or not the wound becomes infected, whether or not he can stand a fever.' He shrugged. 'I've seen men with worse wounds pull through and I've seen others with minor ones die.' He reached for the whiskey. 'Bill seems a tough old bird and I'd reckon that he'll pull through.' He took a mouthful of the raw spirit. 'That is if we can get him back to the fort and Doctor Andrews.'

Bill groaned and stirred a little. Terrance supported his head and held the canteen to his lips.

'Drink deep, old timer,' he said gently.

'What happened?' Bill made groping motions with his hands.

'Take a drink and you'll feel better.' Terrance held the canteen as the old man gulped at the whiskey. 'It's all over.

'I mean that the arrow's out and that you're going to be all right.' Terrance gave the old man another drink, took one himself then passed the empty canteen to the sergeant. Gilcross took it, tilted it and glared as he found the whiskey gone. Sweeny chuckled as Terrance handed him the small knife. He cleaned it against the sole of his boot and tucked it away in its special hiding place.

'Operation finished, Terrance?' Major Perlis walked towards the little group.

'Yes, sir.' Terrance rose and brushed himself down. 'We can tie him on the stretcher and he should be able to make it back to the fort without too much danger.' He hesitated. 'He said that the Harrisons were all dead. Indians.'

'Is that true?' Perlis stared down at

the old prospector. Bill nodded.

'True enough,' he said, and told the major what had happened. 'It's my guess that they've been raiding all through the hills,' he said. 'The Harrisons were killed some time yesterday and Jud first thing this morning. I doubt if you'll find a miner alive in all this part of the Blanca Hills.'

'We've got to be sure.' Perlis frowned in indecision. 'Gilcross, what's your opinion?'

'If the Comanche have been raiding then Bill's right,' said the sergeant deliberately. 'They would have swept through the diggings collecting hair. If they did that then it's my guess they'll be preparing for an attack on the fort. We should let the colonel know what's happened.'

'They may only have attacked these two mines,' pointed out the major. He eased his crippled leg. 'In that case the rest must be warned to return to the fort.'

'I could warn them,' offered Gilcross.

He elaborated. 'A big party like this can't move without attracting attention and, begging the major's pardon, the men ain't what you'd call used to Indian fighting. I reckon that I could get round a lot faster and a lot quieter on my own!'

'If you were caught it would mean a horrible death,' pointed out Perlis. 'I can't permit you to go into the hills alone.'

'Better one than all of us,' said Gilcross. 'This patrol would be like sitting ducks to Indians in ambush.'

Perlis nodded. It was a problem and one that had to be solved. His orders were plain, to ride to the diggings and order the miners to accompany him back to the fort where they would be safe. If they had not rescued the old prospector things would have been simple, but now, aside from the raw, ill-trained men under his command, he had to think of the injured man.

He looked at his command. Half of them were the volunteers, and, aside from Sweeny and Terrance, seemed as much at ease in this hostile land as did the other men. Gilcross knew the area while the rest did not. And it was important that the news of the raiding be carried back to the fort.

He made his decision.

'I can't allow you to go alone,' he said. 'But what you say is true. Choose two men to go with you, make a quick trip and scout and report back as soon as you can.'

'I'd prefer to go alone,' said Gilcross.

'Maybe, but that is impossible.'

'Not for me,' argued the sergeant. 'I know this territory and I can get by.' He laughed. 'Hell, major, I've hunted and scouted every inch of these hills. I don't need no nursemaids.'

'You will take two men with you, sergeant,' snapped Perlis. 'Those are orders.'

'Yes, sir.' Gilcross shrugged as if he knew best but had to obey. He pointed to Terrance and Sweeny. 'I'll take these two, sir.'

'Anything else you need?'

'Some rations, ammunition and water.' Gilcross stared about him. 'And horses, sir, naturally.'

'Naturally.' Perlis had not missed the sarcasm. 'On your way then, sergeant. I'll expect you back at the fort in two days.'

He stared down at the other, acknowledged the salute and then went to supervise the loading of the injured man.

Gilcross grinned at the two men he had chosen.

'You fancy this trip?'

'I've always wanted to see the world,' said Sweeny. He walked to his horse, adjusted the girths and changed his canteen for a full one. Terrance did not answer the sergeant. Instead he checked his ammunition and loosened the pistol in its holster. Unbuckling the long sabre at his waist he handed it to one of the men returning to the fort.

'You better take this cutlery. Throw it on my bunk, I shan't be needing it.'

'You've got sense.' said Gilcross. 'I was waiting for that.' He unbuckled his own sabre and, after a second's hesitation, Sweeny followed suit.

'Can't move quietly with that thing clanking all over the place,' said Gilcross. He shook his canteen and frowned. 'You shouldn't have used all the whiskey. One of us may get bitten by a rattler and then we'd need it.' He shrugged. 'Well, can't be helped. Let's get out of here before the major bawls us out for not being properly dressed.'

He led the way to the horses.

8

It was hot in the hills. The sun beat down from the bowl of the sky like a molten sphere of brass sending little heat-shimmers from the rocks and the harsh dust, wilting the sparse vegetation which defied the lack of water and good soil as it grew from cracks and crannies in the stones. A lizard darted across a boulder, its eyes like tiny jewels, and a rattler, coiled in the sheltering coolness of a shallow cave, lifted its head and sounded its rattles in warning as three horsemen passed by well out of range of its poisoned fangs.

'Hot,' said Sweeny. He mopped his face. 'Now I know why preachers always warn us about Hell. Get the sinners up in these hills and they'd sure see the light.' He spoke dully as if not really interested in what he was saying but merely talking in an effort to break the silence.

'Dead,' said Gilcross. He spat at a stone. 'Every one of the diggings empty and the miners dead. All of them down to the last man.' He could not seem to get over it.

'Indians?' Terrance knew but he asked just the same.

'What else?' Gilcross spat again. 'Damn foolish question.'

'Was it?' Terrance stared at the scarred sergeant. 'I know a little about Indians and I've never known them to turn robber yet. They steal, sure, horses and food and blankets and anything useful they can get their hands on. But gold? Never known an Indian who cares about gold yet.'

'What you thinking, Terrance? Renegades?'

'Could be.'

'Sure it could.' Gilcross knew that white men had dressed as Indians in order to pass the blame for their depredations on the tribes. He also knew that white men had deserted their own race in order to fight with their Indian friends. 'But we bumped into a group of them back where we rescued Bill. They weren't Renegs.'

'No,' admitted Terrance. He frowned. 'Strange about the gold though. In every digging we searched the gold had been taken. In some cases the miners had been tortured and it's a fair guess to say that whoever tortured them wanted to know where the gold was hidden. You agree?'

'Keep talking.' Gilcross rode easily in the saddle, his alert eyes flickering about him as he spoke. The old Indian fighter was ready for any danger and, though he seemed to be totally relaxed and almost half asleep, yet he could spring into instant life. He had proved that a few miles back when he had whipped up his rifle and shot the head from a rattler which had darted towards his horse.

'How much gold would you say was produced in these diggings? How much would you guess the miners would keep by them?'

'Hard to say.' Gilcross screwed up his face in thought. 'To hear them talk you'd think that they only operated their mines for the sake of keeping their hands busy, but that's natural with miners, they just don't like to let on how high their pay dirt assays.'

'Is it high?'

'High enough for waterless stamp mills to show a profit. Jud and Bill used to pan a stream and I know for a fact they used to find some pretty big nuggets. I guess they took about a couple of ounces of dust a full day.'

'The others about the same?'

'More or less. The Harrison diggings produced more but he had his three boys to help him.' Gilcross rubbed his chin. 'The fact is,' he said, 'the miners hadn't been into town at all this summer. Most of them came out in spring and have been working at their claims ever since. That means they had accumulated a tidy heap of dust between them, maybe a hundred thousand dollars worth, maybe more.'

'As much as that?'

'Maybe more.' Gilcross helped himself to a fresh chew of tobacco. 'Safe enough,' he said to Terrance's inquiring expression. 'With Indians about a man daren't smoke or chew. They can smell the smoke for a mile and a chewer spits and leaves a trail. But there ain't no Indians around here now.'

'What makes you so sure?'

'No traces. No horse droppings. No smoke signals.' Gilcross spat. 'They came into the hills to get the miners. They got them and they've gone back to their wigwams.'

'I hope you're sure about that.' Sweeny was nervous. He had been nervous ever since he had seen the fire-blackened fingertips of one of the dead miners. Death, to him, was one thing, torture was another. He rubbed his stomach. 'When do we eat?'

'We'll camp up on the peak,' said the sergeant. 'Good view from there and we can check the country. After that we can head towards the fort and give Austin the news.'

They camped on a rocky bluff bare of vegetation and, despite the sergeant's statement that there were no Indians in the vicinity he would not allow a fire. They ate cold, chewing lumps of fat bacon, hard tack biscuits which seemed made of sawdust and swallowed the unappetizing meal with the aid of tepid water in their canteens. Gilcross scowled at a worm-eaten biscuit.

'Some army contractors should be shot,' he said. 'We pay good money for rotten food.' He flung the biscuit aside. 'Better still, they should be made to eat their own rubbish. I wouldn't ask a dog to live off the rations we get.'

'I've eaten worse,' said Terrance grimly. 'You want to try the slop they dish out in a prison camp.'

'Who dishes out?'

'The glorious Army of Liberation,' said Sweeny. He sneered. 'Damn blue bellies. I wish I had me a rifle down in

Virginia and a bunch of the swabs in front of me. They wouldn't take me a second time, man I promise! I'd rather be lynched than gaoled.'

'Maybe so.' Gilcross remained calm. 'Me, I wouldn't know. I ain't a Southerner nor a Northerner. I'm like the colonel, a Westerner. Seems to me that when they get through with that foolishness back east they can get together to do the real job.'

'Which is?' Terrance was interested.

For answer Gilcross gestured to the country around them.

'Settling the West, you mean?'

'What else? There's land a plenty just waiting for a plough. Grass enough for all the cattle you could imagine. Wood for houses and water for stock. It's good land, all of it, and all just waiting to be settled.'

'And what about the Indians?' said Sweeny. 'I don't figure on settling no land when I might wake up one morning to find my head without a scalp.'

'That's why it's important to get rid of the devils,' said the sergeant. 'The colonel knows more about that than I do.'

Sweeny grunted, not answering, and stared moodily over the rolling hills. Gilcross spat and then looked at Terrance.

'You was an officer, wasn't you? A captain, right?'

'That's right.'

'He's still a captain,' said Sweeny. 'A captain in the Confederate Army.' He glared at Gilcross. 'And I'm a sergeant.'

'Who's arguing?' The sergeant touched the scar on his cheek. 'A peddlar fixed this up for me. Sewed it real neat after a drunken Indian had tried to cut me to streaks with a scalping knife. I got the Indian but he left half my face hanging down like the dewlap on a dog. The peddlar used a bit of sinew and a needle and he soused it in whiskey just like you did to Bill. It sure hurt but it healed real good.'

'Alcohol sterilizes the wound,' said

Terrance absently. 'The rotgut you drink in these parts is almost pure grain alcohol.'

'That's how I guessed you knew some doctoring,' said Gilcross. 'Was you a doctor?'

'I'd almost finished medical school when the war broke out,' explained Terrance. 'Most of what I know I learned the hard way, in the field. The military hospitals offered plenty of scope to anyone willing to learn.'

'That right?' The sergeant shrugged. 'I guess so.' He stared towards the horizon. 'Old Doc Andrews is getting past it,' he said. 'Takes longer to dig out a bullet than any man I know. Maybe he'd take kindly to an assistant.'

'Not interested.' Terrance stared over the hills. They were part of the Blanca range and this was the first time he had been among them. 'Know a place called Herman's Gorge?' he said casually.

'Herman's Gorge?' Gilcross frowned. 'Seems familiar.' He snapped his fingers. 'Sure, I know it. Herman was a

Dutchman who once got himself chased by Comanches. He ran like his tail was on fire until he came to the canyon. He couldn't go back so he tried to jump over. Almost made it, too, and would have made it if an arrow hadn't caught him in mid-air. They found his bones about a month later and his partner, a trader by the name of Whistle, told what happened.'

'Why didn't they kill Whistle too?' Sweeny stared at the sergeant over his shoulder. 'It's a hell of a name, anyway.'

'He was touched,' explained the sergeant. 'The Indians don't go after anyone who's touched. He used to whistle all the time, that's why they called him Whistle.' He sighed. 'Must be twenty years ago or more since I saw him last.'

'About Herman's Gorge,' said Terrance. 'Where is it?

'That way.' Gilcross pointed. 'About ten miles, southwest. See those peaks, the three of them? Well, the Gorge is just past them a little way.' He rose and stretched himself. 'Guess we'd better get moving.'

He led the way to the horses and they recommenced their ride to the fort. Terrance began to fall back, letting his mount slow down and, when he noticed what the captain was doing, Sweeny fell back too. Gilcross, after waiting for them a couple of times, swore and jogged ahead. If the snotty Southerners wanted to be alone he was not going to wet-nurse them. It was safe enough, no Indians for miles, and he was eager to get back to the fort and the cache of whiskey he had hidden.

'Herman's Gorge,' said Sweeny significantly. 'Old Zebe's mine.'

'I'm going to take a look at it,' said Terrance. 'You ride ahead with the sergeant and I'll swing from the path. Cover me for as long as you can. I'll make good time and will meet you back at the fort. Understand?'

'Can't I come with you?'

'Someone's got to stay with the sergeant.'

'You sure that you'll be safe in the hills all alone?' Sweeny eased his collar. 'Don't forget them miners and what the Indians did to them.'

'Gilcross says that there are no Indians around this part of the mountains. I'll be all right.' Terrance dragged at his reins. 'Get moving now and cover up for me.'

Sweeny saluted and rode ahead. Terrance, turning his mount, galloped swiftly back down the trail and towards the three peaks leading to Herman's Gorge and old Zebe's fabulous claim.

For a while he rode in fear that the sergeant would overtake him but, in this, he was mistaken. Gilcross was impatient to get back and it was almost sunset when he learned that the captain had left the party. He cursed in both English and Comanche, then shrugged. Terrance was a grown man and knew what he was doing. If he wanted to stick his head into danger then that was up to him. He would have to answer for his desertion to the colonel when he returned to the fort.

Terrance rode swiftly but carefully along narrow trails and between frowning faces of blank stone. The path wound and twisted so, at times, he was heading in all directions of the compass. But he had memorized his bearing and, no matter how the trail wound back on itself, managed to keep heading towards the place he wanted. He rode in an unbroken silence. No animal made its cry or bird moved across the sky and, aside from the rattle of stones beneath the hooves of his mount, he might have been a dead man in a dead world.

He shrugged off the feeling and, to reassure himself, checked the carbine at his saddle and the pistol at his waist. A few hours' hard riding and he passed the three tall peaks in the shape of a triangle swinging the head of his mount so as to ride directly towards the setting sun.

The trail to Herman's Gorge was a shallow canyon, dusty and rock-strewn.

He rode until the trail ended at a deep, narrow canyon and he guessed that this must be the gorge. Returning down the trail for about two miles he searched the path to his right and found another, almost unrecognizable trail which widened as he left the gulley behind him and began to climb into a nest of small hills looking like a jagged set of teeth against the blood coloured sunset. He rode for about four miles and then halted, staring around him with searching eyes.

The place was barren, devoid of life, a world of stone and dust and emptiness. A man could get lost in these hills and die of thirst. He could wander for days until driven insane by loneliness and heat. Terrance was not going to get lost or go insane. He was looking for two hills which reflected the setting sun in the colour of fresh-spilt blood.

He found them almost at once.

They were to the west, two tall peaks and, as they caught and reflected the rays of the setting sun they literally shone. It was the quartz in them, Terrance knew, the crystalized quartz heavy with veins of gold that had given the hills their name. The Red Hills, an apt title. He rode towards them.

The gulley old Zebe had mentioned was a shallow gash weathered between the two red peaks, the site of an old watercourse long since dried up. A tiny shack rested against one of the peaks, a tottering thing of a few planks and stone weighed canvas, the whole rotten with the passage of time and the fury of the summer suns. Some ashes, cold and long dead, marred the whiteness of the stone and a couple of rusty tin cans, the receptacle of meals eaten in the distant past, had rolled against one end of the shack.

Terrance stared at them, recalling old Zebe and the way he had died, the message he had whispered and the life he had led. He shrugged and dismounted, looking for the gold the old man had claimed was to be found.

The captain was no miner but he knew something of geology and prospecting. He knew that the mother lode, the main seam of which the other diggings were merely offshoots, could run under the ground for a long distance, sometimes buried deep as in the famous Cornstock diggings, and at others, by some prehistoric upheaval, thrusting itself above the surface.

The hills, heavy with quartz, were such an upthrusting.

With a heavy stone Terrance hammered some of the mineral from its resting place. He held it between his hands, pursing his lips as he saw the thin threads of gold streaking the quartz. It was high grade ore and would assay at a respectable figure. He smashed it between heavy stones, making a crude stamp mill to powder the mineral and separate the precious metal. Such mills were always used in any mine where there was a shortage of water. The ore was crushed, riddled and passed over sieves, the heavy gold sinking through the mesh to the bottom of the debris.

Rising from the heap of shattered quartz Terrance stared about him. The gulley had once been a water-course running between the red hills. That meant that, at one time, gold must have been washed from the rock by the action of erosion. The captain began to walk down the gulley, his eyes searching the ground at his feet. He found a small nugget almost at once.

It was about the size of a bullet, a shapeless mass of heavy metal dull in the brilliant sunshine. He picked it up, weighing it in his hand and felt excitement mount within him.

Zebe had spoken the truth. This area was rotten with the yellow metal and it was so easy to mine that a few men could tear a fortune from the rock within a short time. They would need supplies, food and water and pack mules together with canvas sacks to transport the gold, but it could be done. It would be done. Up to now

Terrance had thought of the gold as a remote possibility. His main purpose in volunteering for Austin's special corps had been to escape inevitable death during the coming winter. Locked in the warehouse, the conditions being as they were, Terrance knew that none of the prisoners would have survived.

But the gold was here and he had thirty men back in the fort who would obey his every command. Thirty men would be ample to work the mine, the fort held all the supplies he would need and given a few weeks, he could send a pack train loaded with gold down to the money-starved South where it could be turned into cannon and guns to beat back the advancing North.

He smiled as he thought about it.

The sun was sinking beneath the horizon and the twin hills seemed as though painted with blood. Terrance began to search for more gold, eager to collect a sizable amount now that he was here. He wandered further and further from his horse, kicking at the rocks and picking up nugget after nugget. He took off his hat and had almost two pounds of raw gold in the improvized container when instinct screamed a warning.

He looked up to see a painted devil rushing towards him, tomahawk raised and flashing in the sun.

The Indian moved as silently as a ghost, no shrilling war whoop to terrify the enemy, no yells or other sounds. His soft moccasins flew over the rocks, his copper skin gleamed in the sun and, even as Terrance watched the bright blade of the tomahawk swung towards his unprotected skull.

Desperately he flung himself away from the swinging weapon and, as he moved, he flung the hat with its heavy load of gold directly at the painted face of the Indian. His aim was true, the metal smashed into the painted face and the Indian, for the first time, made a sound. He shrieked the blood-curdling war whoop of the Comanche as he fell, his broken nose adding further colour to his grotesque markings.

It was answered from just around the hill. Terrance ran towards his horse, his hands clawing at the pistol at his waist. An arrow whipped past his head and another shattered on the stone at his feet. Again came the war whoop and, as the captain tore the pistol from its holster, two Indians raced towards him. They came running, one from each side, lances in their hands and blood-lust gleaming from their eyes. Terrance sprang to one side as a lance darted towards him, fired, thumbed back the hammer and fired again, the echoes of the shots rolling in man-made thunder from the hills. He twisted, felt the stab of a lance in his thigh, levelled the Colt at the second Indian then stumbled over a loose stone.

He fell, his elbow smashing against the ground with numbing force, the pistol flying from his hand. Frantically he grabbed for it with his left hand, his fingers curving around the butt just as something crashed against his head and filled his vision with stars and mounting blackness.

Oblivion closed around him.

9

Painted Horse caressed the repeating rifle in his hands and stared into the leaping flames of the council fire. Around him, in a solemn circle, sat the elders of the tribe, all dressed in their ceremonial robes, their impassive faces turned towards the fire, their legs crossed and their hands resting before them. Bent Twig, the Shaman, looking like something from the world of nightmare in his buffalo skin robe and his carved and painted mask, stamped and danced around the edge of the council circle, a gourd rattling in his right hand and a bunch of fresh-cut twigs in his left. He was dancing the dance of the propitiation of the evil spirts, frightening them away so that the elders would be able to think with clear thoughts and speak with straight tongues.

He finished the dance with an elaborate rattle of his gourd and wavings of the bunch of twigs. The gourd was to summon the good spirits, the twigs to snare the evil and, as he spun to a halt, he flung the twigs into the fire so that the heat of the flames would send the evil influences far from the council.

Painted Horse sighed as a man sighs who is heavy with thoughts. From his side he lifted a pipe, carved from stone and painted with many figures. He lit it from the fire, took three solemn puffs and passed it to the warrior at his right. The pipe passed around the council, each man taking his three puffs and, when it had gone the full circle, Painted Horse placed it beside him on the ground. The pipe of peace had been passed, the Shaman had assured good influences, the Council was about to begin.

'The white trader has brought us many of the new guns,' said the chief slowly. 'He has taken our gold and given us the rifles of the white men.'

'Has he also given us the bullets for these guns?' Red Dog scowled at the fire. 'Guns are useless without the bullets to put into them. They are like a bow without arrows, a spear without a head. They are for children, not warriors.'

'Some bullets has he given us,' said Painted Horse. 'Many are to follow.'

'I trust not the white trader,' said an old and wrinkled elder. He looked almost lost beneath his heavy robe but his coup feathers showed that, when young, he had been a great and mighty warrior. Coup feathers, to the Indians, were what heraldic devices were to the white men of a bygone age, but with one difference. Where a shield or coat of arms could be inherited, coup had to be won. A feather was allowed for being the first to kill an enemy in battle, for collecting the most scalps, for touching an enemy with bare hands, for killing an armed foe without weapons. Each feather told a story of valour and a warrior with many coup was respected and admired for, as all men knew, he had won them with the strength of his arm and his own personal courage. And Indians considered personal courage to be the highest of the virtues.

'The white trader worships gold,' muttered Painted Horse. 'He will do much for gold. He has brought us many of the guns which shoot many times and, in that, he has kept his word. We have given him more gold as I promised to bring still more guns and bullets.'

'Why did he not bring the bullets with the guns?' Crazy Mule held out his wrinkled hands to the fire. 'It is not a good thing for us to trust the enemies of our people.'

'He will bring the bullets,' said Painted Horse. His hands stroked the rifle. 'He wants the yellow stone and will do much to possess it.'

'He is a fool,' said Red Dog. 'Can a man eat the yellow stone?'

Painted Horse sighed, not answering.

The Indian indifference to gold or to personal wealth other than horses was a part of their way of life and could not, immediately, be changed. The chief knew of the power of gold when dealing with the white men. He knew that a little of the heavy metal could buy much food and many blankets. He knew of the prospectors who risked their lives and suffered incredible hardships to glean the yellow stone. But to the warriors such work was foolishness and the gold but a plaything for children.

'The warriors have roved the hills and killed all the white men who dig our land for the yellow stone,' said Red Dog. 'They have collected many bags filled with gold as you asked them to do. For these bags they expect the new guns and many bullets. They talk bad words against Painted Horse and they still have no guns.'

'That is the purpose of this council,' said the chief. He paused and stared from face to face. 'With the new guns one warrior will be as many warriors,' he said. 'The Long Knives do not have these guns, only we have them. It would be well for us to wait until the white trader returns with more guns and many bullets. Then we will give each warrior a gun and so will attack the fort and sweep the Long Knives from our land.'

It was White Man's strategy he was talking and the Indians couldn't understand it. Planning, discipline, tactics, were, to them, outside of their experience. Their way was the natural way, a yelling charge and a flurry of battle, kill or be killed, then a retreat to count their losses, burn their dead and claim their coup. That was the Indian method of waging war, more a blood-thirsty game than anything else, and it was what had made them wither before the attacks of the white man. For the Indians could not fight for long. Each raid was, to them, a war, and when over forgotten.

But the white man did not forget and

fought until his enemy was utterly defeated.

'Your words are good words,' said Red Dog. 'I walk with you. But the young men are not children and they have collected the yellow stone as you asked. They will think highly of Painted Horse if he gives them the guns.'

It was not a threat but the threat was there and Painted Horse knew it. A chief remained a chief only as long as he was permitted to remain in that position. He could give no orders which the warriors did not wish to obey. He could command only because the tribe were willing to follow him because of their respect for him as a person. A chief who ignored the wishes of his tribe was in turn ignored.

The warriors wanted the guns they had earned. They would have them.

Later, when the council had broken up, Bent Twig, devoid of his ceremonial robes, walked with the chief of the Comanche.

'The ways of the Indian are not the

ways of the white man, my brother,' he said. 'The warriors are not as the Long Knives who are as slaves to those who are over them.'

'They are as children,' said Painted Horse bitterly. 'They go their own way while the lands of our fathers are stolen from us. They fight, yes, but they fight not as a single arm and a single spear as do our enemies.' He sighed and shook his head as if to clear it from ugly visions. 'How fares the white man?'

'He is brave.' The Shaman led the way to the edge of the village. 'For two days now he has had no food, no water, and yet he cries not.'

'That is well.' Painted Horse halted and stared down at the man at his feet. 'That is very well.'

Terrance opened his eyes and stared at the grave features looking down into his own. He blinked, thinking that he was dreaming, then fought down the impulse to beg for water. Since he had woken in the Indian village life had become a jumbled nightmare. The blow on his head had given him a slight concussion so that, even when conscious, he had raved and not been wholly sane. He had slept much, waking only to feel the stab of pain in arms, legs and head.

He was staked out at full length on the ground, his arms and legs tied with rawhide, his face and body unshielded from the sun. The side of his head ached from the blow which he had received in the Red Hills and the wound on his thigh, minor though it was, burned as though drenched with acid. His uniform tunic and shirt had been cut from him and his naked torso was burned to a painful redness.

'His eyes are clear,' said the Shaman. 'Manitou brushed him but lightly.'

'It is well,' said Painted Horse. 'Those who are Of Manitou may not be harmed.' He prodded Terrance with the toe of his moccasin and spoke in his slow English. 'You know where you are?'

'In Hell,' croaked Terrance.

'You are in the village of the

Comanche.' Painted Horse didn't understand the captain's terminology. 'You were taken in the sacred place of blood. Why did you go there?'

'A man needs water before he can talk,' said Terrance. He licked his cracked lips with his swollen tongue. The gesture was unmistakable.

'Give him water,' said Painted Horse.

The Shaman stooped, picked up a gourd and allowed a thin trickle of water to pass Terrance's lips. The captain gulped at it, straining upwards as if to reach the gourd then relaxing as he felt the bite of the thongs around his wrists and ankles.

'Enough.' Painted Horse stared dawn at the white man. 'Will you talk?'

'Why not?'

'Release him, his hands only.'

Terrance winced as a sharp knife severed his bonds. The pain of returning circulation stabbed at his hands, swollen and numb from their long confinement. The Shaman helped him to sit upright, then, as he snatched at the gourd, knocked it away.

'Later,' he said. 'You talk first.'

'What do you want to know?' Terrance rubbed his wrists and carefully touched the side of his head. His concussion had gone and his thoughts were clear. The exposure to the sun had, luckily, not caused sunstroke though, when he visualized what could happen to him he wished that he had remained in delirium. An unconscious man felt no pain.

'You were in the sacred place of the Hills of Blood,' said the Shaman. 'Why did you go there?'

'I was lost,' lied Terrance. 'I became separated from the others and was trying to find a way back to the fort. 'I wandered to where you found me.' He licked his lips. 'I didn't know that the place was sacred.'

'The spirits of the dead dwell in the hills,' said the Shaman seriously. 'At the end of day just as the sun sinks towards the sea, they return to show all men their wounds.'

'I see.' Terrance nodded, his face thoughful. It was logical enough from the viewpoint of the superstitious Indians. The setting sun reflecting from the quartz was an unusual sight in this part of the world. It would be natural for the Indians to invent a legend to account for it.

'I did not know that the place was sacred,' he said carefully. 'I meant no harm.'

'The yellow stone,' said Painted Horse. 'Where did you find it?'

'At one of the diggings,' said Terrance. It was a lie but the best he could think of. The Indians must know that there was gold close to the Red Hills but they did not know that he knew. They also knew that gold was the one sure magnet to attract the white prospectors. If news ever got out that their sacred place was a bonanza then they would be overrun with gold-hungry prospectors who would think nothing of exterminating the tribe so as to get to the precious metal. The prospectors would come, the Indians would kill them, then the cavalry would arrive in force to sweep the Indians away from the lands they had hunted for generations.

'He lies,' said the Shaman in Comanche. 'The yellow stone was loose and carried in his hat. The warriors saw him collect it. He speaks with a forked tongue.'

Painted Horse nodded, his face impassive. A liar, to the Indians, was even worse than a coward.

Terrance stared up at the chief. He was in trouble and knew it but his head, still aching from the blow which had knocked him out, throbbed with his dream of a victorious South. The gold he had found on old Zebe's claim must be mined and sent to where it would do the most good. For a moment he toyed with the idea of using the Indians to help him but dismissed it almost at once. They were a race apart and would never sell themselves for gain. Even if he could bring himself to use them against the North he would fail. Then he remembered the tortured prospectors and remembered also that he was a white man. A renegade was hated and despised by both sides.

'What are you going to do with me?' he said.

'You are our enemy and you will die.' Painted Horse stared hard at the prisoner hoping for some display of fear. He was disappointed.

'A man can die but once,' said Terrance.

'A brave man can die but once,' corrected the chief. 'A dog can die many times.'

'So you know that quotation too?' Terrance shook his head. 'Never mind, I guess you don't know what I'm talking about, but in some things we think alike.' He drew a deep breath. 'Well, you painted devils, if you're going to kill me get on with it.'

Painted Horse heard his words and understood them. His knife flashed as he cut Terrance free and gestured to the

177

warriors lounging around the village. They snatched at the white man and dragged him to a stake sunken upright in the dirt. They tied him so firmly that he couldn't move and then, slowly, they began to dance around him.

'Torture.' Terrance licked his lips and wished that he could have a drink. Clinically one part of his mind wondered just how much pain he could stand while the other watched the preparations going on around him. He sweated as he remembered tales told of Indian torments and remembered that Bill had sworn to kill himself rather than be taken prisoner. He wondered if, given the chance, he would kill himself, then forgot it as a warrior ran towards him.

The brave wore no paint as he was not on the warpath but he held a tomahawk in his hand. The sunlight flashed on the blade as he swung it at the helpless man's head and Terrance felt the coolness of the steel as it thudded into the post a fraction from his ear. Another warrior repeated the gesture, a third, a fourth, then they snatched out their weapons and made room for a man with a bow and arrows.

'He shows no signs of fear,' said the Shaman to Painted Horse. 'He knows how to die.'

'Wait.' The chief gestured and the warrior with the bow fitted an arrow and drew it back to his ear. Terrance watched him with a strange detachment.

It was the wound, he thought, the blow on the side of his head which made him so calm. The Indians, the village, the hot sun all seemed to belong to the world of dreams so that none of it was real. The tomahawks hadn't been real and, even as they had hissed close to his face, he had not felt afraid.

If they struck then he would die, somehow he knew that, but death was, to him as to most men living a normal life, something remote, and always happening to someone else. Even while part of his mind examined the results of a hit from an arrow, the other part reminded him that, as yet, he had felt no pain and, even if an arrow struck, would feel little. He knew enough of medicine to know the results of a barbed head tearing into his flesh. The arrow spun and the wide head would rip and tear at muscles and tissues. There would be shock and a great loss of blood and a tearing agony. Then, if the loss of blood and shock were great enough, he would die. If the arrow struck a vital organ it would be as quick and as effective as a rifle bullet. If not then he might linger for a while in pain. But in either case an arrow wound was no worse than a bullet wound.

The warrior fired the first arrow.

It didn't hit though it had seemed to be coming directly towards his face. Terrance felt a slight shock as the wide head embedded itself in the stake, the shaft so close to his cheek that he could feel it by moving his head a little to one side.

A second arrow lanced towards him.

A third. More. All hissing as they cleft the air, all thudding into the stake, all nearly hitting but all missing by a fraction. The Indian was a good shot.

Terrance closed his eyes and relaxed. His senses swam so that the noises of the Indians watching seemed to recede, to become as the washing of the sea, the surging of distant water. He smelt the heavy, sickly scent of pale magnolias and heard the singing of the field hands as they gathered cotton, the thick, white tufts of snowy cotton from the fields around the big house.

'He is dead.' Painted Horse halted the shooting of the arrows.

'Not dead.' The Shaman touched the relaxed man. 'See, he is still breathing.'

'Wake him.' Painted Horse shook his head. Never had he seen a man fall asleep beneath the torture. Most men, even some Indians, cringed and screamed as the arrows lanced towards them, victims of their own imagination.

Terrance opened his eyes as the Shaman shook him, annoyed at being woken from his memories. He stared about him, at the village, the Indians, the strong sunlight. A smell rose from the place, the reek of rancid animal grease and body odours, of musty hides and sun-scorched dust. The light hurt so he closed his eyes again, forgetting the present in memories of the past. Of the huge bales of fresh-cured tobacco in the warehouses at Richmond, sweet with the tang of molasses, golden brown and representing, with the white cotton, the wealth of the South.

He woke again to find himself stretched out on the hard ground, rawhide thongs at wrist and ankle, the sun blazing down on his naked torso.

'Drink.' The Shaman held the gourd to his lips and poured lukewarm water down his throat. Terrance gulped, tried to grab the gourd and felt the tug of the rawhide holding him down.

'You are with Manitou,' said the Shaman. He gestured upwards. 'His eye is upon you. It may be that you will return to the world of men and then we shall put you to the fire-death. But if it be as Manitou wills and his touch rests with you then you shall be freed to wander as you will.' He poured more water from the gourd. 'But first you must be tested. You will stay as you are until it is to be seen if you are of Manitou or are of the world of men. Water shall be given you at the rising and setting of the sun. This I have promised.'

'Thanks.' Terrance croaked the word, his tongue like leather. Part of his mind, the sane part, guessed what had happened. His indifference at the stake had prompted the Shaman to claim him as having been touched by Manitou, of being off his head. In that Bent Twig was correct: concussion, exposure and the searing heat of the sun lifted Terrance into a shadow-shot world of delirium.

The captain closed his eyes again, forgetting his physical misery in pleasant memories, not feeling the sun as it burned down, the ants which tore at his

183

flesh, the flies settling on his face. Around him squatted a circle of Indian children hoping for diversion for, to them, the spectacle of an enemy prisoner screaming out his life was common. They, in turn, were perfectly ready to die in the same way.

The sun burned its way across the sky, evening fell, the night closed in and stars blazed in the heavens. The children went to their evening meal and to sleep in the wigwams, the cooking fires died and the watching guards gathered about their fading warmth. The prisoner was ignored, left to live or die as the spirits saw fit, and the talk of the Indians was all of the new rifles handed out by Painted Horse rather than the sick and tormented man at the edge of the village.

Terrance opened his eyes. It was cold, the chill night which comes so fast in the mountains, and his almost naked body shivered at the touch of the keen wind. Something rustled close to him, the same sound which had jerked him awake, and he thought of snakes and coyotes come to bite and tear at his helpless flesh.

His head was clear, more clear than ever before, and things stood out in the starlight with remarkable clarity. He guessed that he had passed the crisis, his medical training telling him what had happened. The concussion, the delirium, the sunstroke, had passed, leaving him weak and exhausted but in his right mind.

Something touched his right wrist. Something cold and hard. He twisted his head, frantically, and was about to shout when a hand was clamped over his mouth.

'Not a sound. It's me, Gilcross.'

The knife touched Terrance's left wrist.

'Rub your wrists and get them working again.' The sergeant crawled down towards the captain's ankles. 'That's better. How do you feel?'

'Terrible.'

'That's no wonder; you'll feel worse

still when the blood starts running.' The sergeant crouched beside Terrance. 'Don't move for a bit, you'll only stumble all over the place.'

Terrance sucked in his breath as agony burned along his limbs. The rawhide had cut deep and, now that the blood was circulating again, it felt as if hands and feet had been dipped in acid.

'Take a drink.' Gilcross handed over a canteen. 'Not too much or you'll get the belly ache. Sip slow and swallow gently. That's enough.' He snatched away the canteen.

'Hadn't we better get moving?' Terrance rubbed his wrists and ankles. 'They may not like what you're doing.'

'I've scouted the village,' whispered the sergeant. 'The Indian who is supposed to be watching you ain't in no condition to watch anything.' He peered towards the fires. 'The rest are too busy with them new guns of theirs.' He growled deep in his chest. 'Wait until the colonel hears about this.'

'How did you find me?' Terrance was

more concerned with the main problem.'

'Tell you on the way to the fort. Ready?'

'I think so. Got a pistol?'

'Could you use it if you had one?'

'No.' Terrance moved his fingers. 'I guess not.'

'Follow me then and move slow and quiet. Sweeny's waiting with the horses. We'll have to ride double but I guess we can manage.'

The sergeant, as he slipped away, was a shadow moving among the shadows. Terrance waited until he had reached a patch of scrub and then followed him. Time halted as he moved so that he didn't appear to be making any progress. He felt naked and vulnerable as he crawled from the stakes, expecting that any moment an Indian would shout the alarm and come rushing towards him. It was with relief that he entered the scrub and felt the sergeant's hand on his arm.

'So far, so good.' Gilcross stared back

the way they had come. 'Not much danger if we don't make a noise,' he whispered. 'Them Indians rely on their dogs and guards. The guard is dead and the dogs are too busy eating buffalo meat to worry.' He spat. 'Half-starved dogs will eat before they bark and anyone who feeds them is their friend.'

'You've done this before,' said Terrance. 'Crept into an Indian village, I mean.'

'Sure, lots of times.' Gilcross smothered a chuckle. 'Nothing to it if you know how to move quiet and kill without noise. I took five horses off old Great Bear once and helped the colonel from a fire-party a few months later.' He edged further away from the village. 'Come on now, and don't breathe unless you have to.'

Sweeny and the horses were waiting several hundred yards from the village. A dead warrior, his face ghastly in the starlight, lay sprawled against a stunted tree. Gilcross stooped over the body and straightened with a rifle and a mass of something dark in his hands.

'Evidence,' he said grimly. 'The colonel likes to be sure of his facts.'

'Let's get moving,' whispered Sweeny. 'This place gives me the creeps.'

'All right, but we'll have to walk for a while.' The sergeant passed his burdens to Sweeny and took Terrance's arm. 'It'll hurt you but you've got to walk. Unless you limber up you won't be able to sit a horse or use a gun and we may have to do both.'

It did hurt. It hurt like the fires of hell and sweat streamed down the captain's body as he forced his numb legs and dead feet to support him. Sweeny led the horses, his hands on their muzzles to prevent them whinnying, and, as they moved away from the village, some of his confidence returned.

'You all right, Captain?'

'Thanks to Gilcross.' Terrance bit his lips as he mumbled. 'How did you find me?'

'Simple.' The sergeant spat a stream of tobacco juice. 'At first I was minded to ride straight to the fort but then I saw Indian signs and made Sweeny tell me where you'd gone. That part of the mountains is sacred and I guessed that you'd run into trouble. So I scouted round and watched the village.'

'Just like that?'

'Well, we had to take some precautions,' admitted the sergeant. 'The moon was up last night so I couldn't get you then. I thought we'd lost you when they tied you to that stake and started having fun. Then Painted Horse began to dish out them new rifles and the braves was as tickled with them as a kid with a box of candy. I guessed that tonight would be the best time to try and get you out of the village.' He shrugged. 'Seems as if I was right.'

'Thanks,' said Terrance. He shuddered at recent memories. 'I guess that I was part-way out of my head.'

'Lucky you were,' said Gilcross. 'You fit to ride now?'

'I think so.'

'Better wear this.' He stripped off his

tunic. 'Manage?'

'Thanks, but I'd rather not.' The touch of the rough fabric was torture to Terrance's sunburned flesh. 'I'll make out.'

'You wear it,' insisted the sergeant. He peered at Terrance. 'Sore?'

'You could call it that.'

'I've got some grease.' Gilcross dug into his saddle-bag and produced a pot of reeking ointment. 'Bear grease,' he explained. 'Best stuff for bone-aches I ever saw. Here, rub it all over.'

Terrance gritted his teeth as he smeared the thick grease over his burned skin but, after he had done so, he could wear the tunic without too much discomfort. Gilcross helped him into the saddle, swung up behind him and nodded to Sweeny.

'Let's go.'

Together they rode through the night towards the safety of the fort.

10

Colonel Sam Austin sat at his desk and studied his maps in the soft glow of an oil lamp. It was night and from the firing platform surrounding the stockade, he could hear the steady footsteps of the guards as they patrolled up and down, their boots thudding against the wooden planking. It was a comforting sound, warming with the knowledge that armed men were on watch ready to beat back any attackers but, as he thought of the troops under his command, the colonel felt a growing despondency.

They were good men and they meant well but they were raw troops when they should have been experienced men.

Indian fighting was learned from experience, not from a few weeks on a barrack square. The men could load, aim and fire their rifles and knew the elements of drill but that was all. Most of them had not as yet fired a shot in anger, felt the quick terror as bullets whined towards them or the soul-numbing fear inspired by the war whoops and the painted faces of the Indians around them.

The Confederate volunteers were better. They were battle-hardened men and knew how to hold their fire until their shots went home. But they were in the minority, a third of his force, and, despite the oath they had taken, there was still friction between them and the men of the Union.

Austin sighed as he straightened from his maps. He had some good men, Gilcross, Sweeny, Terrance, a couple of others, but his second in command was more eager to get back east than to make a life for himself in the new lands, and still imagined that Indian wars could be fought with the training he had received at West Point.

Outside the footsteps of the guards broke their rhythm as the new detail took over. Austin glanced at his watch, surprised to find it so late. He thought of bed then dismissed the idea; his brain was too active for sleep. Taking a cigar from a box on the table, he lit it from the lamp, belted his revolver about his waist and, taking his hat, stepped from his office into the night.

It was clear as only Western nights can be, the stars shone so bright and looked so close that it was hard not to reach up and try to touch them. The air, chill as ever in the mountains, held the sweet scent of sage and a faint breeze cleared away the last traces of the burning day. Austin drew at his cigar, enjoying the night, then turned as a shadow came towards him.

'Perlis?'

'That you, Colonel?' The major rubbed his aching leg as he halted beside the tall man. 'I've just been checking the sentries.'

'Everything all right?'

'Yes.' Perlis glanced about the compound of the fort. Like most of its kind it was built of thick logs with a firing platform running below the parapet. From the centre of the compound a watch tower reared itself into the sky and, against the inner walls, rested the bunk shacks, the cabins containing stores, living quarters, kitchens, stables and all the offices and other buildings necessary to military life. In one corner a well had been dug and filled buckets stood in various positions about the compound.

'How about the men?'

'Morale, you mean?' Perlis shrugged. 'As good as can be expected.'

'How good is that?' Austin was sharp but he kept his voice low. 'Has that blue belly-Johnny Reb nonsense stopped yet?'

'Does it matter?'

'It matters a great deal.' Austin drew at his cigar in order to control himself. 'We are a fighting force and can only be efficient while the men work, fight and are willing to die together. Feuding and hate must be discouraged and stamped out. Here we have no blue bellies or rebels. We have soldiers. I want you to remember that.'

'I'll remember it,' said Perlis.

Austin stared at him. 'Forgotten something, Major?'

'I don't think so.' Perlis frowned.

'I am your ranking officer,' reminded Austin coldly. 'Familiarity can be overdone. I will accept it from a man who is as good, or better than I am, no matter what his rank. But not from you.'

'Do you mean that I'm not as good as you are?' Perlis almost choked with rage. To think that this frontier-soldier had the temerity to abuse him, a graduate of West Point!

Austin shrugged. 'I say nothing, Major,' he said evenly. 'But you expect the men to address you as befits your rank. I expect the same. Do you understand?'

'Yes.'

'Yes, what!'

'Yes, sir.' Perlis stared at the colonel.

'But there's one thing . . . ' The rest of what he was about to say was drowned out in the challenge of the sentry.

'Halt! Who goes there?'

'Who do you think?' The voice echoed from the darkness. 'If we was Comanches, sonny, you'd be a pincushion by now. Didn't anyone ever tell you to watch outside and not inside the fort?'

'Advance and be recognized.'

'Sergeant Gilcross and troopers Sweeny and Terrance,' said the sergeant. 'And two horses. Now open that gate and let us in.'

The heavy wooden portals swung back and two tired horses stepped within the compound. Three men dismounted, moving stiffly and a little awkwardly. One of them staggered and almost fell.

'Tell the Colonel we have news for him,' said the sergeant. 'Move!'

'I'm here, sergeant.' Austin stepped forward, the red point of his cigar a living coal in the darkness. One of the sentries carried a lantern and, by its light, he stared at the travel-weary men. 'I expected you back days ago. What happened?'

'We were delayed,' said Gilcross. 'Indian trouble.' He rasped his hand across his chin. 'With the Colonel's permission, we haven't eaten for two days. Would the Colonel permit us to eat and wash before making our report?'

'Certainly.' Austin turned to Perlis. 'Have the cooks prepare these men a meal. Issue tobacco if they need it.' He touched the sergeant's arm. 'Trouble?'

'Could be.' Gilcross licked his lips. 'But it'll keep for an hour. With your permission, sir?'

'Granted.' Austin watched as the three men staggered towards the bunkhouse.

Terrance didn't speak as the others helped him inside. For two nights and a day he had been wracked with pain, jolted on the saddle and parched with thirst. His body still burned with a raw soreness and he reeled with weakness. He almost fell on to the edge of his bunk. Sweeny stripped off the tunic and whistled as he examined the captain's body.

'Maybe we should get the doc to have a look at him?'

'Bear grease will work better than any sawbones,' said Gilcross. He rummaged in his duffel bag. 'Bear grease and whiskey.' He found a canteen, unscrewed the plug, took a long drink and wiped his mouth. 'Sure needed that. Here.' He passed the canteen.

The whiskey was raw, almost pure alcohol, but it warmed and filled Terrance with new strength. He took a second drink and then, crossing to the washhouse, laved his head, face and body with soap and water. It hurt but he welcomed the pain. It cleared his mind of the last traces of his head injury and refreshed him almost as much as the whiskey. Returning to the bunkhouse he smeared his torso with grease, donned a soft shirt and put on his spare uniform. By the light of a lantern he shaved, clipped the hair from around the scalp wound and deliberately drenched it with a little whiskey.

'Man, you sure hate yourself!' Gilcross had also washed and changed his clothing, knowing that a man who looked good felt good. His eyes were red with lack of sleep but his thick-set body showed no signs of fatigue. 'What's the idea?'

'I want to get fit fast,' said Terrance. He took another drink of whiskey. 'What you going to tell the Colonel?'

'Just about the Indians.'

'And me?'

'We can say we parted, you got jumped and we saved you.' Gilcross stared up at the ceiling. 'Don't seem much sense in telling him you deserted from the party and took a gander at the Red Hills.'

'You know?'

'Sure I know. I back trailed you, me and Sweeny, and found where you'd been. We found your hat and a smear of fresh blood on a rock. The sign was plain.'

'And you aren't going to tell the colonel?'

'He's got enough to worry about.' He broke off as Sweeny came in from the wash-house followed by the major.

'Your meal is ready,' snapped Perlis curtly. 'Report to the colonel as soon as you have finished.' He threw a packet of tobacco on the nearest bunk. 'Hurry now.'

'Yes, sir.' Gilcross picked up the tobacco. 'Right away, sir.' He spat on the floor as the major left them. 'Damn stuffed shirt,' he said. 'The colonel would make ten of him and still leave enough over for a real man.' He climbed to his feet. 'Let's get ourselves some chow.'

The food was rough but wholesome. Bacon, beans, corn bread and hot, strong coffee. They ate like starving men. Terrance not realizing how hungry and starved for food he was until he commenced eating. He wiped the last of his meal with a scrap of bread, refilled his tin cup and rolled himself a cigarette from the package of tobacco Perlis had given them.

'The colonel's a patient man,' he said wonderingly. Anyone else would have had us in his office for questioning as soon as we arrived.'

'The colonel's got sense,' said Gilcross. 'He knows that the first thing a tired and hungry man wants is food and coffee. Then he can collect his thoughts and talk sense instead of just babbling the first thing that comes into his head. Anyways, I told him that there wasn't no great hurry and he can trust me.'

'You mean he knows he can trust you,' corrected Terrance. He drew a lungful of smoke. 'Strikes me that Austin is a man who thinks of others.'

'He's done his share of scouting and doing without,' said Gilcross. 'A man like that tends to forget his braid and remember that he's a man first and an officer second.' The sergeant took a fresh chew of tobacco. 'Austin's one man I'd ride to Hell and back for,' he said simply. 'And if I knew that I wasn't coming back I'd go there anyways.' He spat and climbed to his feet. 'Meet you at the office.'

Terrance nodded, finished his coffee and led the way towards the colonel's office. He knocked, the door opened and Austin gestured them inside. He was closing the door when Gilcross, carrying the rifle he had taken from the dead Indian, appeared. He swung the rifle in one hand and something dark in the other. Terrance hadn't yet seen it at close quarters; Sweeny had carried it during the ride back to the fort. Gilcross grinned when he saw the captain staring at it.

'Ain't you never seen a scalp before?' He pressed into the office and put it, together with the rifle, on the table. Austin sat, helped himself to a cigar, offered them around and gestured to chairs.

'Sit down and get the weight off your

feet.' He waited until they were comfortable, then stared at the sergeant. 'Report.'

'We rode out to warn the prospectors,' said Gilcross. 'The major must have told you about that.' He thought of something. 'How's Bill?'

'Dead.'

'Dead?' Terrance half rose to his feet. 'But how? He was all right when I left him.'

'Major Perlis ran into a little trouble,' said Austin drily. 'A couple of Indians took a few shots at him and winged one of his men. He decided to return to the fort at full speed. The sick man was dead on arrival.'

'Haemorrhage?'

'So Doc Andrews said.' Austin stared at his cigar. 'He also said that your operation was a masterly piece of work. A pity that it was wasted.'

'That Perlis!' Gilcross had liked the old prospector. He remembered who and what he was and contained himself by an obvious effort. 'Sorry, colonel, but me and Bill were side-kicks one time. It seems strange to think that he won't be around no more.'

'I understand.' Austin changed the subject. 'Major Perlis sent you to warn the miners. What happened?'

'We found them dead,' said the sergeant simply. 'All of them.' He touched the scalp. 'This came from an Indian I killed. He was carrying it in his belt. It's a white man's hair and it's not old. My guess is that it came from one of the Harrisons.'

'Could be.' Austin picked up the grisly trophy and examined it. 'Fresh and taken in war. A white man's right enough.' He dropped it back on the table, his face serious. 'So they wiped out the miners. Know why?'

'I can make a guess.' Gilcross picked up the rifle. 'You ever seen one like this before, Colonel?'

'You take this from an Indian too?'

'The same one.'

Austin nodded, examining the repeating rifle. He stared at it, operated the lever, read the name on the barrel.

'A Winchester. I've heard of them but thought that they were all due for the army.' He put down the weapon and stared at Gilcross. 'Tell it.'

Gilcross told it. He explained how the three men had gone from mine to mine and, at each place, had found the miners dead, everything of value taken from the cabins and the gold they had mined and readied for shipment gone. He told how while on the way back to the fort, Terrance had lost his way and been attacked, how he and Sweeny had followed the trail and effected the rescue. He spoke simply, using a bare minimum of words and yet giving every essential detail. When he had finished Austin sat, smoking, his face furrowed with thought.

'What made you leave the others, Terrance?'

'I'd dropped behind and must have taken the wrong trail,' said Terrance easily. 'The country's pretty broken in that part and it's easy to get lost. A couple or more Indians jumped me. I shot one, but the other hit me a crack on the head.' He touched the place where he had clipped away the hair. 'When I came to I was staked out in an Indian village.'

'So you got lost.' Austin stared at the three men, his eyes lingering longest on Terrance. 'Is that your story, Gilcross?'

'Yes, sir.'

'And you are sticking to it?'

'That's right. Colonel.' The sergeant took a puff at his cigar. 'Lucky it turned out as it did in a way. If it hadn't we'd still be in the dark about the rifles.'

'Yes, the rifles.' Austin picked up the weapon and examined it again. 'This is new by the look of it, no signs of wear and still bearing traces of the grease it was packed in. A brand new weapon straight from the factory.' He operated the lever to ensure that the gun was empty, lifted it to his shoulder and pressed the trigger. The hammer fell with a dry click. Austin immediately re-cocked the gun and fired again. He went through all the motions of rapid fire and, when he replaced the gun on the table, his mouth had thinned to a tight, hard line.

'Repeaters,' he said grimly. 'Better rifles than we have and in the hands of the Indians.' He slammed his fist on the table. 'Repeaters, by God! And us still with single shot carbines. Those Comanches can fire seven shots to our two. What do the army think they're playing at?'

'Maybe they didn't want the guns,' suggested Terrance. 'There's no law against a man buying rifles if he wants to.'

'Admitted, but how would an Indian get to the factory to buy them?' Austin picked up his discarded cigar, puffed at it, scowled when he found that it had gone out, then relit it.

'Gold,' said Terrance thoughtfully. 'That's what gets me worried. What would Indians be doing with gold? They normally don't want it and yet, from what we've seen, they went on the warpath merely to kill the miners and rob them of their dust.'

'That's right,' said Gilcross.

'Sure is.' said Sweeny.

Terrance picked up the rifle.

'An Indian wouldn't know how to go about buying a gun,' he said slowly. 'All he knows is what he learns from traders. Traders are interested in furs and hides and gold. Supposing . . . '

'You think a white man sold the guns to the Indians?' Austin was sharp. 'Is that it?'

'It could be the answer. These guns must be expensive, nothing like the old army surplus rifles or trade guns the Indians normally buy. They are a brand new model, even the army hasn't been issued with them yet.'

'The army gets what's going last,' said Gilcross. 'Right, Colonel?'

'Near enough. But we would have known about these weapons had they been available for long. Prospectors and traders would have them even if we didn't. They value their skins more than the few extra dollars it costs to buy a decent weapon. The Navy Colt proves that; the army, as usual, has only just been issued with them and yet they have been around since the start of the war.' He shook his head. 'But a white man? Selling these guns to the Indians?'

'Why not?' Terrance was cynical. 'A lot of men will do a lot for gold — providing there is enough of it. How else would the Indians have got these guns? They would have to be collected by a trader and delivered to Painted Horse. And the murder of the miners proves that the Indians wanted their gold. Gold to pay for more guns.'

'The swine!' Gilcross clenched his big hands. 'The dirty renegade!'

'It seems clear enough,' said Austin. 'Some trader has entered into an agreement with the Indians to supply them with guns and ammunition in return for gold, nuggets collected over the years and kept as sacred stones or even as playthings for the children.' His face darkened. 'But the trader would know how to get gold. Damn him. He as good as killed those miners for the sake of profit. He's more to blame for their deaths than the Indians are.'

'I'd like to get my hands on him,' said Gilcross. 'I'd teach him to deal with the Comanches and sell them guns to kill the white men. Good guns too, better than we've got.' He looked at the colonel. 'Sir.'

'Yes?'

'May I request the colonel's permission to go on a scout to find the louse?'

'No, sergeant.'

'But, sir!'

'Request denied!' Austin softened. 'I know how you feel, sergeant, and I sympathize with you, but we have more important things to worry about right now than some renegade trader.' He picked up the rifle. 'Now that the Indians have these what do you think they will do with them?'

'Use them, I suppose,' said Gilcross. He swore deep in his throat. 'They'll want to use them at target practice with us as the targets.'

'Exactly.'

'Do you think that they will attack the fort?' Sweeny eased his collar. 'Is that it, Colonel?'

'What else?' Austin threw down the weapon and rose to his feet. He rested his hand against a map on the wall. 'Look at the map. Here is the fort.' His finger jabbed at the painted surface. 'Here are the Blanca Hills and here is the Indian village. We are surrounded by Indians and they all hate the white man. More, they think that they have us on the run. They know as well as we do that this fort is garrisoned with inexperienced men. If I were Painted Horse I'd be getting ready to attack as soon as my warriors had learned how to use the new rifles.'

'That won't take long.' said Gilcross sombrely. 'They was playing with them when I lifted Terrance from the village.'

'Then they may be waiting for either more guns or more ammunition. They can't repeat the raid on the mines and so have all the gold available. The trader, whoever he is, must have taken it to buy the rifles and ammunition, or perhaps he will collect it as a reward for selling out his own race or . . . ' Austin shrugged. 'What does it matter? The Indians have the new repeaters. We are sitting here like a bunch of fish in a barrel. All Painted Horse has to do is to pick his time.'

'Should I make a scout?' Gilcross looked hopeful. 'I reckon that I could do some damage if I went about it the right way.'

'What could you do?' Austin answered his own question. 'You could kill a few Indians, maybe burn a few wigwams and steal a few horses. You'd do fine, I know it, but you'd be one man fighting an Indian Nation. They'd get you, Gilcross, never fear they wouldn't. No matter how good you are, how careful, they'd get you in the end.'

'Maybe.'

'There's no maybe about it.'

'I ain't boasting,' said the sergeant. 'But I went in and got Terrance out and we came here without trouble. What I did once I can do again.'

'Not yet, you can't,' snapped the colonel. 'The Indians are aroused now. They will have missed their prisoner and are probably ringing the fort at this moment. You'd never get through and, even if you did, I still want to keep you here.' He strode up and down the narrow office.

'I need every man I can get, sergeant, and you're worth twenty of the others. You know the Indians, what they will do, how they think, a dozen things. You can save this fort by that knowledge but you can't do it if you're not here when the attack comes.'

'Attack?' Sweeny looked at Terrance. 'You sure about that?'

Austin didn't answer.

'Sure there'll be an attack,' said Gilcross. 'May come at dawn or may come in a couple of days.' He heaved himself to his feet. 'With the colonel's permission I'd like to get some sleep.'

'A good idea.' Austin passed his hand across his eyes and sat down behind his desk. 'All of you get some sleep.'

They left him staring at the rifle.

11

The next two days were a time of waiting. Tension mounted higher as the burning sun dragged its way across the empty sky and the nights, brilliant with stars shielded the jagged peaks of the Blanca Hills. Every man in the fort was conscious of the Indian menace and young, untried soldiers nervously fingered their rifles as they stared towards the hills watching for the painted devils they had learned to fear.

Sweeny worried the most. He was a man used to the scream of shot and shell but he had seen what had happened to the miners and, like many brave men, while he did not fear death and combat, he feared the tortures awaiting if he fell into the hands of the Comanche.

And he had seen gold.

He had heard Zebe's whispered

instructions, all but the latter part, and he had followed Gilcross into the mountains to the Red Hills where Terrance had been attacked. He had said nothing but his sharp eyes had seen the quartz, the handful of spilled nuggets and the tell-tale signs of a bonanza. He had spoken to Terrance about it the morning after their return to the fort.

'Did you find it?'

'Find what?' Terrance had stared at the man.

'Zebe's mine, the place you were looking for.' Sweeny had lowered his voice. 'This is what we volunteered for, ain't it? To get out of that prison and to get our hand on some guns.'

'In a way.' Terrance glanced upwards to where the flag of the Union hung in the still air. Once the sight of the stars and stripes would have filled him with rage, with the burning resolve to tear it down and replace it with the stars and bars of the Confederacy. Now, some-how, he no longer felt the same burning fanaticism as he had.

'Well?' Sweeny glanced over his shoulder. 'What we waiting for? I've sounded out the men and there are about twenty-five we can trust. We can rise at a word and take over the fort. With the blue bellies working for us we can work the mine and load up with gold for the South.' His voice deepened. 'Say the word, Captain, and the thing is done.'

'No.'

'Why not, Captain?' Sweeny stared from beneath his eyebrows. 'You're still for the South, ain't you?'

'Of course.'

'Then what you waiting for?'

'We're surrounded by Indians,' said Terrance evenly. 'If we take over the fort as you say then we'll be less than thirty men against all the Comanche. And don't forget that the Indians are armed with repeating rifles. We wouldn't have a chance of beating them off. We need every man we can get on the firing platform when the shooting starts and, even if we did take over, we couldn't do other than give them back their guns to help us save our own lives.'

'You think that they will attack, Captain?'

'The Indians?' Terrance shrugged. 'Sure.'

'What makes you so sure?'

'This fort is the only garrison in this area. If they destroy it then they will think that they have swept the white men completely from this part of the mountains. More, once Fort Ambrick is gone there will be no troops to protect the prospectors and settlers crossing the range. You saw what happened to the miners, would you like it to happen to others?'

'No.' Sweeny swallowed. 'What chance you think we got, Captain?'

'Here in the fort?' Terrance looked doubtful. 'I don't know. Most of the men are green, our men are the only really experienced troops here aside from Austin and Gilcross. We may be able to beat them off.'

'I hope so.' Sweeny scowled at the sentries on the firing platform. 'And what about the gold?'

'We'll wait.'

They had been waiting for two days and two nights and during that time Sweeny had done a lot of thinking.

He was not happy and said so to the other Confederate volunteers.

'We're sitting cooped up in here like fish in a barrel,' he said on the third day. 'Everyone knows the Indians are going to attack the fort and with repeating rifles, too. You know what will happen then?'

'What?' Lawson, a big Virginian, looked at the speaker.

'Austin will put us up on the firing platform to fight his war for him, that's what.' Sweeny spat thoughtfully on the ground. 'Know why?'

'Tell us,' urged Lawson. 'What's on your mind, Sweeny?'

'Sergeant to you, Lawson.'

'Like hell.'

'I'm a sergeant,' snapped Sweeny.

'The same as Terrance is a captain and don't you forget it. We ain't resigned from the Confederate Army just because we volunteered for this outfit. We had to get out of that prison, didn't we? Well, an oath extracted under duress ain't no valid oath. A lawyer told me that once and I guess it applies to us the same as anyone else.'

'You sure?' Young was from Texas and looked it. 'About the oath, I mean.'

'Sure I'm sure.' Sweeny registered disapproval of the other's doubt. 'I was speaking to the captain about it only the other day and he said that it was right. He said so back in that warehouse. You think I would offer to renege and fight for the blue bellies else?'

'They ain't so bad,' said the Texan thoughtfully. 'Wet behind the ears still, maybe, but I reckon they'll turn out all right when it comes to it.'

'You ain't told us why we'll be put up top when the shooting starts,' said Lawson. Sweeny nodded.

'It's obvious, ain't it? We're Johnny Rebs and they won't grieve over us if we get knocked over. So Austin puts us up on top and, when we've shot his Indians and got ourselves killed, he'll claim the credit. He may even bury us if we make a good fight of it.' He spat at a crawling insect. 'Why else do you think he got us out here?'

'It makes sense,' said Lawson thoughtfully. 'It sure makes sense.'

'The captain told me that the fort is certain to get attacked,' continued Sweeny. 'The Indians can't tolerate it any longer and so they've got themselves some repeating rifles and are going to wipe it out.' He jerked his thumb towards the stockade. 'Wood,' he said significantly. 'Sun-dried wood. You ever see that kind of wood burn?'

The others nodded.

'You didn't see what I saw,' said Sweeny. 'Men scalped and burned and all cut up with knives. That's what will happen to us, sure as shooting, unless we get shot first or collect an arrow in the gizzard or get fried when they set fire to the fort. And all because of a bunch of blue bellies.' He swore with sudden violence. 'Hell, I joined the army to kill the damn Yankees, not get killed to save their skins!'

He left them then and wandered to another group where he sowed the same seeds of doubt and suspicion. Perlis helped, the major hated to see men idle and, as Austin was catching up on his sleep, he took the opportunity to have the men polish up the compound. He chose at random but it was significant that he chose the volunteers for the dirty jobs. Perlis was a Union man and still had no liking or trust for the soldiers from the Confederate Army.

In return the volunteers gave him their hate and contempt and Lawson, struggling with the quite unnecessary task of polishing the latrine buckets, thought longingly of a dark night, an Indian attack, and Perlis with a bullet in the belly. If necessary he was quite prepared to supply the bullet.

After chow he sought Sweeny and the two men sat with their heads together.

'You've something on your mind, sergeant,' said Lawson. 'What is it?'

Sweeny grinned at the other's use of his military rank. He kept his voice low.

'I don't aim to get myself set up as a clay pigeon, Lawson, do you?'

'Not if I can help it.'

'Good. Now the captain and me's got a plan.' Sweeny glanced over his shoulder to make certain that they were unobserved. 'Listen now, and don't breathe a word unless I tell you.' Rapidly he told of old Zebe dying and passing on the location of his mine. 'That mine's near here, a couple of days' easy ride away. The ground is rotten with the pay dirt, nuggets as big as your thumb just waiting to be picked up.' He paused. 'If there was anyone around to pick them up.'

'A bonanza?' Lawson wet his lips.

'Sure. The captain found it and told me so that I know just where it is.' This was almost true, Sweeny did not think it necessary to tell Lawson that Terrance had not told him or that the captain advised no action at this time. Sweeny used Terrance's authority merely to bolster his own. The main thing of importance was that Sweeny had found the location of the mine.

'What's the catch?' Lawson was impatient.

'It's in Indian country,' said Sweeny. He held up his hand at the other's protest. 'Now wait a minute before you say anything. The Indians are after the fort and won't be watching the Red Hills. Even if they are, thirty of us should be able to take care of any damn Indians, that is if we aren't cooped up behind walls for them to shoot at and burn. Get the picture?'

'I think so.' Lawson sucked in his cheeks. 'Ain't that called desertion?'

'Desertion from who? The Union Army? Hell, I'm a Southerner, the blue bellies are the ones I'm supposed to be fighting. From the Confederates? They won't think so when we arrive at Richmond with a pack train loaded with gold.'

'Yeah,' said Lawson slowly. 'If we arrive.' He looked at Sweeny. The sergeant met his stare.

'Time enough to argue about what we do with the gold once we get it.' he said.

'It's a long way to Richmond,' said Lawson casually. 'A long, long way. Might end up in Mexico if we ain't careful.'

'Why not?' Sweeny grinned and winked. 'That's for later. Now is to get the men out of here so as we can dodge the Indians and get busy at the mine.'

'What do we need and how do we work it?' Lawson, his brain inflamed with thoughts of gold, was all eager to get started. Normally he wouldn't have considered deserting his comrades but, as Sweeny had pointed out, the Union troops were his natural enemies.

And, of course, there was the gold.

'Easy,' said Sweeny. 'Tonight we are

supposed to be on guard, right?'

'That's right.'

'Those who are on duty go through the motions. The rest of us collect water canteens, food and as much ammunition as we can carry. We take guns and sacks for the dust, tools and some blasting powder. We each take a couple of horses and, just when that snotty major comes round, we grab him, give him a tap on the noggin, collect the lads, open the doors and away.' He chuckled. 'Work it smooth and do it right and they won't know what's happened until dawn.' He became serious. 'You with me?'

Lawson nodded.

'Good. Now circulate among the men; do it careful and only talk to those you can trust to be for the idea. They can get the stuff together and we can take the rest of the volunteers with us when we start.'

'And the captain?'

'He stays behind.'

'But . . .'

'The captain,' said Sweeny deliberately, 'is a good Southerner — and he can read a map and plot a route as well as anyone. If he guides the column there won't be no chance of us getting lost.'

'No chance of getting to Mexico, you mean?' Lawson grinned. 'Right?'

'I ain't saying.'

'But suppose they come after us?' Lawson was worried. 'Suppose they send out the captain and he orders us back?'

'They won't.'

'What makes you so sure?'

'Look.' Sweeny pointed towards the horizon. From the hills a thin trail of smoke climbed steadily towards the sky. 'Indian signal. I asked Gilcross what it meant and he says that it means the Indians are calling the warriors to assembly. He said that they'll attack at dawn.' The sergeant whitened beneath his tan at the thought of it. 'We get out tonight, Lawson,' he snapped. 'Or we don't get out at all.'

'And how much gold do you reckon?'

'Depend on how long we can work. If

the Indians stay away and keep the fort busy we should be able to lift a few hundred thousand dollars in dust and nuggets.' Sweeny glanced around the compound. 'Get to work, Lawson. Maybe for you and me the war will be over soon.'

'In Mexico?'

Sweeny nodded.

The day dragged and still the ominous column of smoke lifted towards the sky. Night fell and the tension mounted as the sentries were changed, the more experienced volunteers being given the night watch. Terrance, after walking the platform on his turn at sentry go, retired to his quarters which he shared with Sweeny, Gilcross and other Union troops. He slept heavily, his body still needing sleep to repair itself from his recent hardships, though once, some time towards dawn, he started awake thinking that he had heard a cry. He listened again, heard the steady, measured tread of the sentry, and fell asleep again.

He awoke to find Austin bending over him.

'Terrance! Get up.'

'What's wrong?' The captain flung his legs over the edge of his bunk and rubbed his eyes. It was still early, dawn was barely lightening the sky, and he was due for another two hours' rest.

'Get dressed and come outside.' The colonel was curt and, as Terrance threw on his uniform, he looked for Sweeny. The man was not in the cabin and his bunk had not been slept in.

Outside two men fell in beside the captain. Terrance glanced at them, then at Perlis. The major leaned whitely against the cabin, a rough bandage around his head. He glared at Terrance with undisguised hatred.

'You swine!' he snarled. 'I told the colonel not to trust you damn rebels but he wouldn't listen to me. Well, maybe he will now.'

'What are you talking about?' Terrance looked at the colonel. 'May I ask the meaning of this?'

'The meaning is simple,' said Austin tiredly. 'During the night your men attacked Major Perlis, stole over fifty horses, food, water, weapons and other equipment and have deserted. In the circumstances I have no alternative but to place you under arrest.'

'Arrest?' Terrance looked blank. 'But why?'

'Because you put them up to it, you damn rebel,' said Perlis. The major was almost beside himself with rage. 'You waited until now knowing that we needed every man and then you ordered your scum to desert. You swine!' He stepped forward. shaking with anger. 'Don't you know what you've done? You've condemned every man in this fort to certain death.'

'Every man?' Terrance stared coldly at the major then turned to Austin. 'As an officer and a gentleman,' he said evenly, 'I give you my word that I knew nothing of this. Had I known I should have forbidden it. Those men, as well as I, swore an oath when we joined your special corps. I intend to keep that oath and I intend to see that any other Confederate who took it keeps it also.'

'It sounds nice,' sneered the major. 'Too nice. You slavers were always good liars.'

Terrance took a step forward then halted as Austin grabbed at his arm.

'Stand where you are!' The colonel turned to Perlis. 'That will be enough from you. You forget yourself, I think.' He looked again at Terrance. 'Can you explain this?'

'I don't know.' The captain stared at the hard face turned towards him. In it he read shocked disbelief and a cold hostility. Austin had lost one third of his command at a time when he needed it most and he was in no mood to be gentle.

'Listen,' said Terrance. 'The major accuses me of condemning every man in this fort to death. Is that how you feel about it?'

'If you ordered those men to desert, yes.' Austin made a helpless gesture.

'They deserted just a few hours ago and they left the doors open behind them. We could have all been scalped if I hadn't woken, failed to hear the sentries and risen to investigate. I found the major with a head wound, he had been knocked unconscious, and the volunteers missing. You are the only one remaining in the fort.' He took a deep breath. 'I would like an explanation.'

'First let's be logical,' said Terrance quietly. 'If, as you say, I have condemned everyone in this fort to death then I have also condemned myself. Hardly the sensible thing to do, is it? But I did not order my men to desert and that I promise you on my word of honour. I knew nothing about what had happened until you woke me a few minutes ago.'

'Liar,' said Perlis. 'Dirty, stinking, liar. I . . . '

He broke off, a peculiar expression replacing the look of hatred on his face and, as Terrance watched, he crumpled and collapsed to the stamped dirt beneath.

From his back, rising thin and gaudy in the growing light, the feathered shaft of an arrow pointed towards the empty sky.

12

For a moment they stared at the slender shaft of painted wood, the bright feathers, the thick red mess around the buried head, the peculiar, vacant expression on the face of the dead major. Then something whispered through the morning air, and arrows, lancing from above, quivered in the ground and thudded into the wooden logs of the cabin. From outside rifles sent echoes across the compound and high above in the watch tower the sentry screamed, clapped his hands to his face and toppled from his high station.

The sound he made when he hit the dirt mingled with and was lost in Austin's sharp commands.

'Action stations! On the double, move!'

The Indians were attacking.

They came like a brilliant cloud,

charging across the clearing towards the fort, stooped low over their horses' heads, their coup feathers fluttering with the wind of their passage and, as they rode, sharp echoes and puffs of smoke rose from their ranks together with the deep, throbbing hum of released bow strings. Bullets and arrows fled towards the fort, the bullets splintering the thick logs or whining just above the parapet, the arrows arcing so as to fall beyond the stockade.

'Hold your fire!' That was Gilcross storming along the firing platform his scarred face glistening with sweat as he tried to teach the inexperienced men how to meet their foes. 'Save your shots until they do some good.' He winced as a bullet sprayed his face with splinters from the stockade. 'Damn you! Hold your fire.'

They held it, waiting white-faced as the Indians thundered closer, the sound of their horses' hooves drumming on the arid ground. They waited until the storm of bullets and the whispering arrows grew too much for their strained nerves and then, ragged and ineffective, puffs of smoke lifted from the firing platform as they fired at the Indians and reloaded with fumbling fingers.

'The fools!' Gilcross wiped blood from his torn cheek. 'They're doing nothing but shooting holes in the air.'

Terrance grunted. His arrest had been forgotten in the excitement of the attack and now he was on the firing platform, his Spencer carbine barking as he sent lead towards the enemy. He fired slowly, coolly, taking careful aim and waiting until he was sure of hitting a target before squeezing the trigger. Two dead Indians sprawled on the ground told of the accuracy of his aim.

Austin came past, his lean face anxious as he snapped orders and studied the Indians. Terrance caught his arm.

'Colonel?'

'What is it?'

'The men aren't doing any good firing as they are.' Terrance stared towards the Indians; they had broken their charge and were circling just beyond rifle range. Even though they could not be harmed the raw troops were blazing away at them, shielding the top of the stockade with powder smoke. 'May I take command?' He smiled at the colonel. 'If you can trust me, that is.'

'I can trust you.' Austin made up his mind. Now that Perlis was dead he could obey his own instincts and he both liked and trusted the volunteer. Austin nodded.

'Good. Well, now that's out of the way what about promoting me.' He gestured to the men within the fort. 'Perlis is dead and Gilcross is the only other man who has had Indian fighting experience. I used to be a captain and have seen plenty of action as well as having fought my share of redskins. I can't do much at the moment, the men won't obey me, but if you give me a temporary rank they will.' He stared at the Indians. 'Better hurry, Colonel.

They will return to the charge soon.'

Austin nodded. 'You're a sergeant,' he said. 'That's the best I can do. I'd like to make you an officer but that is beyond my powers. Take sergeant's rank and whip these fools into shape.'

'Cease fire!' Terrance yelled above the sporadic noise of the shooting. 'Hold your fire!' He snatched a rifle from a soldier, pulled another back from the stockade and yelled again at the full pitch of his lungs. 'Cease fire!'

They obeyed, recognizing the iron of command in his voice, the whip-lash of his officer's tones.

'There has been a promotion,' announced Austin. 'Trooper Terrance is now a full sergeant. You will obey him as you would me.'

'Good for you, Colonel!' Gilcross grinned with a flash of teeth. 'Now, Sarge, let's teach these babies how to fight Indians.'

'Right.' Terrance glanced towards the Indians, then at the men lining the stockade. 'Listen and listen good.

Those Indians out there are Comanches, the bravest and most determined of the tribes. They won't be scared and they mean to kill. If they take a prisoner they torture him to death, and I do mean torture. Being buried up to the neck in an ant hill is nothing to what they will think of. I've known a man take three days to die and he was begging for death every moment of the time.'

'That's the truth,' said Gilcross. 'Every word of it.'

'So you mustn't be taken,' said Terrance. 'If you are taken then kill yourselves. If you see a comrade taken then shoot him.' He stared. 'I'm not joking about that. I'll personally kill any man who is captured by the Indians or who refuses to face them. If we're to survive this attack then we've got to fight and win.'

An arrow whispered from over the parapet and buried itself in the planking.

'The Indians are going to charge again soon,' Terrance continued. 'Now remember this; while you are behind the stockade they can't hurt you. No matter what they do they can't get at you until they climb the logs. So don't lose your heads and don't panic. Obey your orders, hold your fire until you are sure of hitting something, and keep fighting.'

He nodded to Gilcross.

'You take the south side, I'll take the west and the colonel can cover the north and east. If my guess is right they'll either attack on the south or west. Detail some men to stand by in the compound with water buckets in case of fire and have the cooks start brewing coffee and prepare a meal. The men can be relieved, one in three or one in four to eat and rest. Tired men make bad shots.'

'Dead men make worse,' said the sergeant grimly. He stared over the parapet. 'Ready! Here they come.'

They came with a thunder of hooves and a hail of lead. They screamed as they charged, the blood-chilling war whoop of the Comanche and their faces, striped and daubed with red and black, green and brown, gave them the appearance of devils riding straight from Hell. Directly towards the west side of the fort they came and Terrance, watching them, felt again the excitement he had so often felt when on a more orthodox field of war when the Union cavalry had charged at his own troops.

Quickly he went along the line of his men, resting his hand on each shoulder and giving each man a number.

'Even numbers fire when I give the word. Odd numbers the same. Each group will fire then drop and reload under cover. Ready?' He narrowed his eyes, gauging distance and speed. 'Aim low now. Aim low, squeeze gently and send the red devils to Hell.'

Bullets whined about him and a man, scarcely more than a boy, groaned and fell, his chest a red ruin. Terrance ignored him.

'Steady number one group. Fire!'

The volley rang out like the crash of doom and a hail of lead and smoke darted towards the charging Indians.

'Number two group. Fire!'

Again the crashing volley and again charging warriors threw up their hands and tumbled into the dust, horses screamed at the hail of lead and wounded men staggered and fell to be picked up by their comrades.

'Number one group. Fire!'

Terrance snapped his commands as though he were on a parade ground, the raw troops instinctively obeying and gaining comfort from the familiar. They felt that the Indians were merely moving targets and they lost their fears as they reloaded, aimed, fired, dropped to reload again. They concentrated on one thing, the mechanical drill Terrance and their training had driven into them, and they fired and reloaded without question, ignoring what was going on around them.

Terrance could not ignore it.

Fire power against fire power the

Indians were superior. They lost much of the advantage in shooting from a moving platform, the backs of their horses, for it is harder to hit a stationary target from the back of a horse than the other way around. But despite that they had superior numbers, superior weapons and a fanaticism the defenders had not yet acquired.

And the Indians were winning.

Seven shots to the defenders' two. Seven bullets to hit the stockade or whine above the pointed logs for every two shots flung at the moving men and horses. Most of the shots fired by the Indians did little more than make holes in the air, but the sheer amount of lead flung at the fort was making itself felt. For the soldiers were careless. They forgot to take cover when reloading, showed too much of themselves when firing and the Indians, used to hunting game and relying on their weapons for food, had great skill in hitting a small target.

By the time the charge had been

beaten back a third of the soldiers were dead or so badly wounded that they were a liability instead of an asset.

'This isn't fun.' Gilcross joined Terrance as the Indians, beaten back, resumed their racing circle, firing at any soldier showing himself and sending arrows winging high into the air to drop within the fort. 'Doc Andrews is dead, an arrow got him as he was tending the wounded. The coloned collected a bullet in the arm, a flesh wound, nothing to worry about. But we've lost a third of the men.'

'The rest will be better for it,' said Terrance grimly. 'Now they know that we aren't playing at target shooting they can be trusted to fire at will.' He glanced up at the sun, surprised to find it high in the heavens. The battle had taken longer than he thought.

'Better tell some of the men to grab some chow and coffee. One out of three, I reckon, and they can fill their canteens and ammunition pouches at the same time.' He looked at Gilcross.

'Any chance of Painted Horse calling off the attack?'

'Not a chance.'

Terrance nodded, the sergeant's opinion was his own. The Indians had tasted blood and had whipped themselves to a fighting frenzy. They could continue the attack for days or, unpredictable as Indians always were, they could retreat for no obvious reason. But with victory in their grasp it was doubtful if they would retreat.

A second charge came as Terrance was snatching some food. He dropped his plate, caught up his rifle and raced to the firing platform. For a time the world was filled with the crack of rifles, spouting plumes of smoke, whining bullets and silent, lethal arrows. A lance flung by some warrior who had ridden almost to the walls of the fort thrust itself from a soldier's throat and he gurgled as he fell from the stockade. Terrance shot the attacking warrior then, as he saw the injured man twitch and some Indians racing towards him, sent lead downwards.

'You killed him!' A white-faced youngster swung around, his rifle pointing at the captain as he turned. 'You shot a wounded man.'

'He was as good as dead!' snapped Terrance. 'And the Indians were coming for him.'

'Dirty rebel!' Terror and tension had done their work on the soldier. 'All this is your damn fault. I've a mind to send you to Hell right now.' He stared at Terrance, his eyes wild in his powder-blackened face and his finger tightened around the trigger of his carbine.

The dry click of the hammer was echoed by the soldier's scream.

He had turned to face Terrance and forgotten the enemy. But the enemy had not forgotten him. His profile had made a perfect target and a bullet smacked into his throat just as he tried to fire his empty rifle at Terrance. He screamed as the pain and shock seared through him, tried to say something then died as blood gushed from his mouth.

Grimly Terrance turned from the dead man and sent lead whining towards the Indians below.

The day passed and the powder-smoke around the fort thickened. There was no wind and the clouds of black smoke coiled and moved as if with a life of its own. It shielded the top of the stockade from the Indians but it tended to blind the defenders so that the Comanche rode closer and closer to the fort as they sprayed the parapet with their repeating rifles.

At mid-afternoon the danger Terrance had been expecting came in the shape of trailing plumes of flame, fire arrows, each shaft bound with grease-soaked rag and each arrow burning as it thudded into the sun-dried wood of the fort.

Men tore them out with their bare hands, stamped on them, threw water on the fires they had caused and coughed at the charcoal odour of burning wood. Together with the fire arrows came another charge and, as evening fell, the toll of dead and severely wounded had risen to almost half the original number.

Gilcross spoke about it as he tore at his food. It was night and, aside from the watching sentries, there were no signs of action.

'Indians don't attack at night,' said the scarred man. 'They don't like to be killed at a time when they can't see to find their way to the happy hunting grounds.' He took a drink of coffee. 'Lucky for us they feel that way. Much more of this and we'd be buzzard meat for sure.'

'How long can we hold out?' Terrance asked. Austin, his arm strapped to his side, answered.

'A day, two days, maybe three.'

Austin shrugged. 'The men are gaining experience the hard way. Tomorrow they will know enough to save their own skins as well as kill Indians.' He sighed. 'But what does it matter? The end will be the same.'

'Maybe.' Terrance stared down into

his tin cup. 'Colonel, unless we can get help we're beaten. Right?'

'Yes.'

'Have you any chance of getting help?'

'None. Fort Ambrick is an isolated outpost. The nearest garrison is over a hundred miles away to the edge of Comanche country. It would be impossible for a man to get there in less than four days, the country is mostly rock and desert. By the time he returned the fort would have been destroyed.' Austin sighed. 'There is no other help in the vicinity.'

'You're wrong, Colonel.' Terrance set down his cup. 'I know where there are thirty men, seasoned fighters, all well armed and with good mounts.' He nodded at the colonel's expression. 'That's right, the men who deserted.'

'You know where they are?'

'I know where they are heading for. I think that I can overtake them and persuade them to return.'

'But . . .'

'I am officially their captain,' reminded Terrance grimly. 'They and I originally belonged to the same army.' He made a gesture. 'Don't misunderstand them or me, Colonel. They believe that they are fighting for a cause, for the South against the North. What they have done they did because of that.' He looked at his hands. 'Maybe I am to blame in part for what happened. It took this attack to show me that there is no South, no North, just white men against a natural enemy.' He looked at Austin. 'With the colonel's permission I would like to go out and find those men.'

'I don't know.' Austin was troubled. 'We need you here, Terrance.'

'You need those men more,' pointed out the captain. 'I am one man, little loss. They are thirty, more than enough gain. With them we could beat off the Indians.' He rose to his feet. 'Well?'

Austin nodded.

13

The night was moonless, lit only by the blazing splendour of the stars and filled only with the sound of his horse's hooves. Terrance sat in the saddle, his every effort strained at speed, speed and yet more speed still. He wore a uniform tunic closely belted around his waist and, in twin open holsters, he carried a pair of Navy Colts.

Escape from the fort had been surprisingly easy. He had waited until the moon had set and then, softly and quietly, the hooves of his mount bound with rags to deaden their noise, had slipped away. Luck had been with him and he ran into no Indians. Later, when sound was less important than speed, he had unbound the rags, settled in the saddle and headed his horse along the path the deserters would have taken, the path to the Red Hills.

It had been luck that he had escaped without challenge. Luck for both him and the challenger, for he would have shot without compunction, killing as many Indians as he could before finally sending his last bullet into his brain. Gilcross, back at the fort, had listened for a long time for the tell-tale sound of shots. Had he heard them then he would have taken his own turn at the ride, running the gauntlet for a second time to appeal to the deserters to return.

But that hadn't been necessary.

The stars paled and the sun rose with a wash of gold and pink, orange and yellow, lightening the east and touching the peaks of the Blanca Hills with liquid gold. The horse stumbled; it was tired after a long, hard gallop, but Terrance could afford to rest neither himself nor the animal.

Noon found both man and horse staggering with utter weariness, the horse covered with foam and stepping along with slow, jaded steps. An hour later Terrance caught up with the deserters.

They were at the edge of the Red Hills, on the path leading to Herman's Gorge. They had travelled slowly and easily, wary of Indians and not too sure of the country. Sweeny, their guide, had wandered from the trail in the darkness and their progress had been slow even though they had pressed on during the night. Terrance joined them, almost fell from his horse and gratefully sucked at the canteen Lawson thrust towards him.

'Glad to see you, Captain,' he said. 'I always said that we shouldn't have gone without you.'

'Why did you desert?' Terrance stared around at the men, then at Sweeny. He stepped forward and faced the sergeant. 'I gave you my orders, Sweeny. I told you to wait. Why did you disobey?'

Sweeny shrugged. Already, in imagination, he was living on the gold torn from the Red Hills, living a life of luxury in distant Mexico. Terrance's arrival had brought him back to earth and he didn't like it. He glanced at Lawson, Young and the other men he had talked into deserting, then squared his shoulders and faced the captain.

'I figured that you'd sold out to the blue bellies,' he said. 'Me, I ain't sold out nor never will. I'm a Southerner and aim to stay that way.' He turned to the others. 'That's right, ain't it?'

They answered him each in their own fashion. Some agreed, some grunted, most looked uncomfortable. They were Southerners, yes, but they were also men and soldiers. Together with their idealism for a cause they valued their personal honour. Sweeny had, by using the captain's authority, persuaded them that in deserting they would be helping the South. They had believed him, believed too that Terrance would approve of their action. Now he was facing them and, obviously, he did not approve.

'You're Southerners,' he said, and the contempt in his voice was hard for them to bear. 'That's what you claim to be, isn't it? Southerners! Well, I'm a Southerner, too, an officer, and I'll tell you this. I don't want to be known as what you are. If you belong to the South then I'd rather fight for the North. You know why?' He glared at them. 'Because you are deserters, that's why. You took an oath and you broke it. Why? Do you know that?'

'We aim to help the South,' said Lawson. 'There's gold here, Sweeny said so, and we're going to get it and take it to Richmond. That's what we're going to do and you ain't going to stop us.'

'No?' Terrance stepped towards the big man. 'You say that you are still fighting for the South?'

'That's right.'

'And you?' Terrance stared at Sweeny.

'Sure.'

'And you? And you?' Terrance stared at them each in turn and each nodded. 'So, as far as you're concerned, you are still soldiers of the Confederate Army, is that it?'

'That's what we said,' snapped Lawson. He looked at Sweeny. 'Tell him, Sarge.'

'We aim to help the South,' said Sweeny. 'Not by fighting Indians for the blue bellies but by doing something real good.'

'Like deserting in the face of the enemy so you can fill your pockets with gold?' Terrance stared at the men. 'The fort was attacked yesterday at dawn, shortly after you left. Half of the garrison is dead. Those boys wouldn't have died had you stayed at your post; they needed your experience and training to help them fight. You killed those soldiers by your cowardice. Yes, cowardice!' Terrance glared them to silence. 'Call it what you will, you deserted the men you swore to fight with.'

'Take it easy,' said Sweeny. 'That ain't no way to talk.'

'I'll talk as I please.' Terrance stared hard at the sergeant. 'As your commanding officer I order you to relieve the fort. You will mount and return with me.'

'No.'

'No?' Terrance narrowed his eyes. 'Insubordination, Sweeny?'

'To hell with that kind of talk!' Sweeny glanced at Lawson. 'We know what we're doing and it don't include taking orders.'

'You're after gold,' said Terrance softly. 'Not for the South despite all your big talk, but for yourselves.' He looked at the watching men. 'If that's what you want then go ahead. But before you can turn yourselves into criminals you'll have to deal with me.' Terrance dropped his hands on his guns. 'All right, Sweeny,' he said. 'You're under arrest.'

'Am I hell!' Sweeny stared at Lawson, then, as the big man nodded, went for his gun.

Terrance shot him between the eyes, turned, shot Lawson just as the big man levelled his Colt. He faced the others, the guns smoking in his hands.

'Still want to find gold?' He looked down at the dead sergeant. 'Sweeny knew where it was but he's in no condition to talk. I know where it is but I'm not going there. I'm going back to where I'm needed most, back to the fort.' He holstered his guns. 'Are you coming with me?'

Their cheer was his answer.

The deserters had taken spare horses and so, with the fresh mounts, they made good time. They rode at full gallop when they could, at little short of a gallop when they couldn't. They stopped twice to rest the horses and snatch some food and rest. At the second halt they checked their weapons and Terrance made plans.

'We'll arrive late afternoon,' he said, staring at the sky. 'We'll travel easy until we get close and then we'll hit them with everything we've got. Shoot fast, hard and often and get them on the run.'

'Sounds easy,' said Young. The Texan rubbed his chin. 'How many Indians did you say?'

'I didn't.'

'All right then, you didn't. But how many are there?'

'Maybe a few hundred,' said Terrance carelessly. He grinned. 'Since when have well-armed, well-mounted Southern cavalry been afraid of a few half-naked savages?'

'Don't give me that savage talk,' said Young. 'We've got Indians in Texas and those Apaches ain't no savages.'

'All right then, forget the savage talk. I remember when we rode against three times our number of Union troops. I don't recall you worrying about numbers then.'

'I ain't worried about them now,' grinned Young. 'Just talking.' He became serious. 'Sweeny shot off his mouth about gold in the Red Hills. Was he telling the truth?'

'Yes.'

'Seems a pity that we've got to leave all that gold lying around.' Young squinted thoughtfully at the toe of his boot. 'What you aim to do about it, captain?'

'The war isn't going to last forever,' said Terrance slowly. 'Maybe the South will win, maybe the North, it doesn't much matter either way. Since I've been out here I've come to realize the foolishness of brother trying to kill brother, white man against white man. It's all so unnecessary when there are all these wide lands just waiting to be settled.' He stared at the majestic hills rising towards the clear bowl of the sky.

'Out here there are no Southerners or Northerners, there are only Westerners and they are a blend of North and South. Here we have men and women who are trying to settle and make a new life, to convert the wilderness into productive land. We have them and we have the Indians who are trying to retain the lands they had always called their own. It's a big problem, Young, and one that must be solved one way or another. Maybe that gold will help solve it. Maybe the South will lose the war and then that gold will help to ease the burden of surrender.'

'Then you aim to mine it?'

'Not me,' corrected the captain. 'Us. Six months after the civil war ends we will be free of our commitments. Then we can turn to mining. But not now, not when the Indians are scalping and killing and burning everything they see. We can't mine with pistols in our hands. Before we can live here in peace we must save the fort, for only that can shield us against the Comanche.' He rose to his feet. 'Time to go.'

'Sure,' said Young. He held out his hand. 'I guess you don't have to be told that Sweeny sweet-talked us into following him?'

'No.' Terrance shook the proffered hand.

'What will happen to us when we get back? Court martial?'

'Maybe, but I reckon Austin will understand.' Terrance grinned. 'A man usually feels kindly disposed to those who've saved his life. The ringleaders are dead, let's leave it at that.'

He reached for his horse.

They arrived at the fort in late afternoon when the sun was on its downward path and the heat of the day filled the air with sticky warmth. The little group of men halted at the edge of the clearing and, as Terrance stared towards the besieged fort, they changed mounts and made a final check of their weapons.

The air was still and the captain could see the puffs of powder smoke rising from the top of the stockade. They were few and irregular; long fighting had reduced the garrison to a bare handful of men. The Indians, made bold by success, rode close around the walls, firing their repeating rifles in an almost continuous blaze of smoke and thunder.

'We'll hit them quick and quiet,' ordered Terrance. 'Ride like the devil straight for them, wait until they spot us and then cut loose with the old rebel yell.' He stared at his tiny force. 'Use pistols and don't stop for nothing. Follow me and, if I'm downed, follow

Young. Ready! Ride!'

His hand swept down and, as a body, the riders struck from cover and headed towards the fort.

They rode as men ride who are born to the saddle, their fresh mounts devouring the distance as they broke from a trot into a full gallop. Beneath them the sunseared grass of the prairie fell away like a brown river and the tiny creaks of leather mingled with the harsh breathing of the men.

Nearer, nearer, nearer until they could see white faces staring at them from the top of the stockade, brown faces staring at them from the backs of Indian ponies.

And then they struck.

Thirty men each carrying two pistols loaded with twelve cartridges and a carbine loaded with one. Thirty men armed with long cavalry sabres and the knowledge of how to use them, mounted on fresh horses and burning for action. They fired as they rode, sending a hail of lead into the circling

Indians, slung their rifles, took their pistols and cut loose with the rebel yell.

It was shocking, that sound. It was something never before heard on the prairie, the strident challenge known on the battlefields of the east and comparing with the war whoop of an Indian for sheer terrifying volume. They yelled and fired as they yelled. They rode like men possessed and the smoke from their blazing guns whipped in the wind of their passage. They hit the Indians and sliced through them, wheeled and repeated the manoeuvre, wheeled again and left a trail of dead and dying to spill their blood on the parched grass.

From the fort echoed a wavering cheer.

'Again!' Terrance signalled with his hand, holstered his empty pistol and drew his sabre, the second gun in his left hand. He yelled, thrust his reins into his mouth and, gripping his horse between his knees, thundered down on a knot of Indians. A lance thrust at him to be knocked aside with his glittering sword. His pistol roared and a warrior, his headdress thick with feathers, tumbled into the dust. He cut, slashed and shot his way through the Indians, the men at his back adding to the carnage as they screamed their defiance at their enemies.

This was the action they loved, the rush of air and the feel of a horse between their thighs, the crack of pistols and the clash of steel, the quick, personal, combat of charging cavalry instead of the boredom of barracks and the sterile battles fought from behind log walls.

Some died, many were wounded, but nothing could withstand their fury. The Indians, shaken by the unexpected attack and the death of Painted Horse, hesitated, screamed their war whoop and then, after a final flurry of shots, rode frantically away from the strange white men who yelled like Indians and fought like devils.

After them rode the Confederate volunteers.

They reloaded as they rode, did those men of the South. They thrust fresh cartridges into their smoking revolvers and fired at painted faces and snarling Indians, blasting until the hammers clicked on empty chambers and their ammunition was exhausted. Then, the bloodlust dying from their eyes, they returned to the fort.

Terrance rode at their head, ignoring the blood streaming from his scalp, the torn uniform and the arrow sticking in his saddle. He smiled as he saw the little band around him, smiled with pride that his men had proved themselves.

Then he rode towards the open gate of the fort where Austin and Gilcross and the rest of the garrison waited to greet him. Not as men of the Union meeting the men of the Confederacy. Not as the North meeting the South, but as man to man, as soldiers, as men with a single purpose and a single country.

Men of the West.

We do hope that you have enjoyed reading this large print book.

Did you know that all of our titles are available for purchase?

We publish a wide range of high quality large print books including:
Romances, Mysteries, Classics
General Fiction
Non Fiction and Westerns

Special interest titles available in large print are:
The Little Oxford Dictionary
Music Book, Song Book
Hymn Book, Service Book

Also available from us courtesy of Oxford University Press:
Young Readers' Dictionary
(large print edition)
Young Readers' Thesaurus
(large print edition)

For further information or a free brochure, please contact us at:
Ulverscroft Large Print Books Ltd.,
The Green, Bradgate Road, Anstey,
Leicester, LE7 7FU, England.
Tel: (00 44) **0116 236 4325**
Fax: (00 44) **0116 234 0205**

THE SAVAGE RIVER

Sydney J. Bounds

The Pinkerton supervisor told Savage that the job was not dangerous. He must find Miss Beatrice Bottomley, a schoolteacher lost in the wild west. But along the way Savage is jailed, hunted by killers and shot twice. All because Bea was abducted by Foxy Parker's gang of gold robbers. But why is she so important to them? Although Savage faces constant danger, he remains undaunted. His guile, courage and expertise have always helped him win through — but will he succeed now?

WYOMING SHOWDOWN

Jack Edwardes

Fifteen years earlier Matthew Granger's father had put his son on a stagecoach heading east. His return to Springwater was solely to settle family affairs. However, his plan to return to Boston as quickly as possible was thwarted by old enemies. Thomas Ralston, owner of the Lazy Y, was taking over the town and settling scores with the Granger family. Matthew Granger was a target again. Strapping on his Navy Colt, he knew Boston would have to wait.

BARBARY COAST GUNDOWN

James Gordon White

A brush with outlaws leads Matt Sutton and Diana Logan to meeting Percy Wilberforce, a private detective from London. He recruits the pair to help him rescue an English countess, abducted in the notorious Barbary Coast district and thought to be in the harem of a Chinese tong leader. A bloody riot in Chinatown, a vicious street gang and a showdown with the tong leader and his hatchet men all lie in wait for Matt and Diana . . .

JUSTICE FOR CROCKETT

Dale Graham

The rivalry between brothers Corby and Link Taggart had boiled over with violent results in the New Mexico town of Cimmaron. Fleeing from the hangman, Corby was pursued by Link, leading him into Wyoming's Yellowstone Valley. There, Link encounters Beartooth Crockett, who exerts a powerful influence on him. So when Crockett is brutally slain, Link determines to bring the perpetrators to justice. The final showdown with Corby and his gang would prove whether blood was thicker than water.

THE NIGHT RIDERS

Matt Laidlaw

Jim Gatlin rode into Cedar Creek hunting the man who had framed him for a crime he didn't commit. Meanwhile, Pinkerton agent Charlie Pine had located the real train robber, a man named Hood. Outlaws Hidalgo, Wilson and River were also after Hood, for the fortune locked up in his home. But why was Marshal Silva making a secret of Hood's whereabouts? Against overwhelming odds, Gatlin would face a bloody showdown, needing all his skill and courage to unlock a shocking secret.

THE LEGEND AND THE MAN

Ben Nicholas

When Morgan headed south across the Rio Grande on an impossible mission, he wasn't alone. No gunfighter turned down the chance to venture into Old Mexico with a legend like Morgan. Ten of them reached the besieged Spanish fortress of Hacienda St Leque, but even before fighting their way in, men were dying at the hands of Colonel Moro and his sombreroed butchers. Many more would fall before Morgan rode out alone to kill the colonel — or die trying . . .